DEAD HAIRY

DEAD HAIRY

Debbie Thomas

Illustrated by Stella Macdonald

MERCIER PRESS
IRISH PUBLISHER – IRISH STORY

MERCIER PRESS
Cork
www.mercierpress.ie

© Text: Debbie Thomas, 2011
© Illustrations: Stella Macdonald, 2011

ISBN: 978 1 85635 678 7

10 9 8 7 6 5 4 3 2 1

Printed and Bound by ScandBook AB

A cord of three strands

is not quickly broken

King Solomon, 900 BC

1

Stuck

Squashy Grandma lunged for her knickers. They slid with a sigh down the back of the radiator. 'Blast!' she tried to say. But it came out as 'Vast!' That was because, as she reached over, her false teeth fell out.

Abbie looked up. Everyone knew Squashy's knickers were vast. Why bother announcing it? 'What's the matter, Grandma?' she said, putting her book down.

'My feef!'

Abbie went over and peered behind the radiator. The teeth grinned up from their flowery knicker nest. 'Dad,' she said, 'Grandma's lost her teeth. And her marbles,' she muttered.

'Marbles,' echoed Dad from behind the paper, 'a truly ancient game …'

Abbie rolled her eyes. *Here we go*, she thought.

'… played two thousand years ago by Julius Caesar …'

Hello? Earth calling History Nerd.

'… who also – interesting fact –'

I doubt that.

'… used to pluck out his body hair with tweezers.'

'Dad –'

At last he put the paper down. 'What?'

'Grandma's teeth are stuck.' Not that there was any point explaining. When it came to practical problems Dad was less use than earwax.

He came over to the radiator. He peered down the back. He rubbed his bald patch. He did his pretend-to-scratch-your-lip-while-picking-your-nose trick.

'Abbie,' he said, 'get the Hoover.'

'You what?'

He did his don't-argue-with-me word jiggle. 'The Hoover, Abbie. Get.'

Shaking her head, Abbie went into the hall and wheeled out the Hoover from the cupboard under the stairs. She dragged it by the neck into the sitting-room like a dog on a lead. Dad pointed the tube down the back of the radiator. He switched it on. Nothing.

'Try plugging it in, Dad.'

The Hoover growled into life. The teeth chatted to the wall.

'Oofeff!' Squashy Grandma got as close to snapping as anyone without teeth can get.

'Not useless, Mother,' said Dad. 'I'm sure it'll loosen them.'

It did. The teeth flew up from their flowery folds. They lodged in the mouth of the vacuum tube.

Dad turned the Hoover off. He shook the tube. The teeth were stuck. He tugged his beard. 'Get the phone book, Abbie.'

'But –'

'Abbie. The phone book. Get.'

Abbie went back into the hall. She knew the numbers of the plumber, electrician and carpenter off by heart. But the Yellow Pages had no Vacuum Cleaner False Teeth Removal man. Between Vehicle Testing and Video Repairs, however, she saw a small advert.

Wobbly widgets? Drooping drains?
Dad less use than earwax?
Call the VERY ODD JOB Man.
075-1345593

Abbie had no idea what widgets were, or how drains could droop, but it sounded promising. She dialled the number.

'Hello. This is Matt Platt,' said a recorded message. 'Please leave your number and I'll c-call you back.'

'This is Abigail Hartley at 25 Mill Street. There's a problem with our Hoover. I'll try again later.' Better keep it vague. She didn't want to put him off.

Back in the sitting-room Grandma was kicking the Hoover. 'Foopid foow,' she spluttered at Dad.

Stupid fool yourself, thought Abbie, gazing at Squashy. *Fancy putting your knickers out to dry in the sitting-room – in full view!* What she said, though, was, 'Poor Grandma.'

Dad grabbed the nozzle and tried to jiggle the teeth out, swearing quietly. Abbie had seen enough. She headed for the kitchen.

It was empty. Perfect. She crept over to the biscuit barrel and stuffed two Bourbons up each sleeve. Then she ran upstairs. She slipped into her bedroom and shut the door. Well, *she* called it shutting.

'Abigail, don't slam!' shouted Mum from her room across the landing. 'I've got a headache.'

Abbie sat down on her bed and eased a biscuit out of a sleeve. She stuffed it into her mouth. Then she took a pocket tape recorder from her bedside table and switched it on.

'GRUMPY GRAN IN HOOVER HELL,' she said into the microphone. 'Squashy Hartley had it coming when she leaned over the radiator to rescue her gigantic pants. The seventy-two-year-old's false tee–'

'Why are you talking to yourself?' Abbie's little brother slid his caramel curls round the bedroom door.

Abbie shoved the tape recorder under her duvet. 'I'll talk to you if you like. Bog off, Ollie.'

'Will you play with me?' he said.

'OK. Grrraaaggh!' Abbie dived for him. Ollie burst into tears and ran into Mum's room. Abbie counted under her breath, 'One, two, three and – wait for it –'

'Abigail! Here. Now,' came Mum's weary voice.

Abbie slunk across the landing. Mum was in bed propped up by pillows. Headache or no, she still looked freshly ironed. Her nightie was smooth. Her lipstick gleamed. Her hair, sleek as custard, hugged her face in a bob. Bob – the perfect name for a perfect style. Abbie liked to think of it as a separate person, smart and fussy.

'Hi Mum,' she said brightly. 'You'll never guess. Grandma's teeth are stuck in the Hoover.'

Mum did her don't-try-to-distract-me sigh. 'What *is* it with you, Abigail? Why do you have to make your brother cry?'

Abbie shrugged. She didn't *have* to, she *wanted* to. Try explaining that to Mum. Try telling her that sometimes it felt good to see his cutie wutie five-year-old face crumple like a crisp bag. And sometimes it felt good to hear his lispy wispy voice wail like a wolf. Abbie didn't *feel* good that it felt good – but it still felt good.

'I only wanted you to play,' Ollie sobbed.

'I did,' said Abbie. 'I was a being a monster.'

Ollie howled. His curls burrowed into Mum's shoulder like worms into earth.

'Darling,' said Mum, stroking his head.

Dung beetle, thought Abbie. What she said, though, was, 'Sorry Ollie.'

'That's better,' said Mum. Abbie got up. A Bourbon dropped onto the bed.

'Abigail. Who said you could – ?' The doorbell rang.

'I'll get it.' Abbie hurtled gratefully downstairs.

***

Outside the front door, Matt Platt stepped back. 'You do the talking, Perdita,' he whispered to his daughter. He nudged her forward. Chitchat wasn't his thing. He'd just fix the Hoover. It shouldn't take long. Just as well. He'd already spent half the morning rescuing a lizard from a liquidiser and he *had* to get home before lunch. Back to his experiment. Because, unless it worked, his darling wife, his precious Coriander, might never come back.

Matt rubbed a dirty finger over his teeth. Ten weeks and three days since Coriander had left – and not so much as a phone call! OK, he'd argued horribly with her. But *surely* she'd forgiven him by now. It was so unlike his wife to sulk. What if she was … No! Don't even think that. He clutched his right plait. He had to hold on to hope.

But if she wasn't … then where on earth *was* she?

***

Coriander leaned on her broom. It felt like a dream, sweeping the floor of this stuffy little room. For the millionth time she prayed she *was* dreaming. But when she pinched her arm it felt horribly real. 'Ow!'

A tear trickled down her cheek. What would Matt and Perdita be doing now? Matt might be inventing some gadget to rescue snails from lawn mowers. Perdita might be trimming the bushes in her gardening trousers. The ones from Tibet made of yak hair. With the hole in the right knee that Coriander had meant to fix … that she might never fix now. Another tear wriggled out.

No! Don't even think that. She clutched her left plait. She had to hold on to hope.

2

Rescue

The first thing Abbie noticed when she opened the door was teeth. Big friendly ones, grinning out from big friendly gums.

The second thing was the girl wrapped round them. She had two black plaits that reached her elbows and eyes that glowed like Marmite.

The third thing was the man behind her. *He* had two black plaits that reached his shoulders and thick glasses. He was clutching a tatty rucksack and rubbing a finger over his own tremendous teeth.

The girl strode forward. 'Perdita Platt.' She grabbed Abbie's hand and pumped it like a piston. 'This –' she flung her arm back, whacking the man in the stomach, 'is my dad, Matt. And this –' she nodded at the number on the front door, 'is 25 Mill Street. So *you* –' she jabbed Abbie's shoulder, 'must be Abigail Hartley. I like your curls Abigail Hartley. They make your head dance. And your freckles. I've always wanted freckles.' Abbie opened her mouth. Nothing came out.

Dad came up behind Abbie and stuck his head around the door. 'Can I help you?'

Perdita frowned. 'I thought *we'd* come to help *you*.'

Dad frowned back.

'The Hoover,' said Perdita.

'The Hoo …' he echoed in a stupid way. Then he slapped his head. 'Oh *right*! Do come in.'

Perdita seized her father's hand and marched into the

hall. She stopped and cocked her head. A furious huffing sound was coming from the sitting-room.

Very slowly Dad opened the door. Perdita followed, then Mr Platt. Abbie came last. She gasped. Both Perdita and her father had a *third* plait dangling from the back of their heads.

Perdita waved across the room. 'Morning,' she called to Squashy Grandma.

'Nnnggh!' Squashy replied, kicking the radiator. Mr Platt edged backwards. But when he saw the Hoover, and the teeth grinning up from it, he couldn't help smiling back.

'That's my Grandma,' said Abbie, 'and those are her teeth.'

'Lovely,' breathed Mr Platt. Abbie could see he didn't mean Squashy. Kneeling down, he stroked the vacuum cleaner like a pet. Then he opened his bag and took out two metal poles. He screwed them together. At one end were claws, like skeleton hands. At the other end was a handle with buttons. Mr Platt pressed one. The claws wiggled.

'The Crookhook,' said Perdita. 'Invented by Dad.'

Mr Platt aimed the Crookhook at the Hoover tube. The claws slipped inside round Grandma's teeth. After more pressing and wiggling the teeth came loose. The claws dropped them onto the carpet, where they beamed up at the world.

'Magic,' said Dad.

Without a word – or sound – of thanks, Squashy swept the filthy dentures off the floor into her mouth. 'Now then young man,' she said to Mr Platt, sucking her teeth into place, 'you'll be so kind as to rescue me undies with that contraption of yours. They're be'ind that radiator.'

Mr Platt followed her gaze. 'Oh *my*,' he breathed, seeing a cobweb on the corner of the wall beside the radiator. He took off his glasses and peered closer. His eyebrows looked as if they'd slipped down each side of his face, making him look even sadder. 'Don't worry,' he murmured, apparently to the spider in the web, 'we'll soon get you out of there.'

'Young man,' boomed Grandma, 'while *you're* chattin' up cobwebs, *my* personals are gatherin' dust.'

Matt wheeled round. 'Shhh,' he whispered, 'you'll frighten the poor thing. Perdita, c-could you get –'

'Sure.' Perdita thumped Abbie's arm. 'Want to come?' It was impossible not to smile back at that goofy grin. Abbie followed her out the front door. An old green van was parked at the kerb. Perdita opened its dented back doors.

'I hope you don't mind me asking,' Abbie said nervously, 'but why have you got three plaits?'

Perdita looked at her as if she'd asked what colour oranges were. 'Because we *are* three Platts. Dad, me and –' she stopped. Her teeth scraped white lines over her chin. 'I hope you don't mind *me* asking, but why are there two biscuits sticking out of your sleeve?'

Abbie blushed. 'Oh. It's, um, a game I play with my brother – Hunt the Snack. Here.' She gave one Bourbon to Perdita and ate the other.

'Thanks.' Perdita munched her biscuit and jumped into the back of the van. 'Now, where *is* that thing?' She rummaged among the spanners and screwdrivers, boxes and bags. 'Ah, there we go.' She pulled out what looked like a red gun and waved it in Abbie's face. 'The Gobbleweb.'

Abbie jumped back. And before she could say, 'The what?' Perdita was rushing back to the house.

In the sitting-room Mr Platt was crouched by the radiator, whispering to the spider. Perdita stood in the doorway. She aimed the gun thing at the cobweb and pulled the trigger. There was a sucking sound, like Grandma drinking tea. The cobweb shot off the radiator, flew across the room and disappeared up the gun barrel.

Abbie shrieked. Dad squeaked. And Squashy straightened her wig, which had slipped over her eyes in the suction stream.

Perdita turned to Abbie. 'Where's your garden?'

Goggling like a goldfish, Abbie led her through the kitchen and outside. Staring like a sturgeon she stood back as Perdita aimed the machine at a bush. And gaping like a guppy she gulped as Perdita pulled the trigger again. The cobweb shot out, complete with spider, and attached itself to the bush.

'Don't mention it,' Perdita said, as if the spider had thanked her. 'Have a good day.' She handed the gun thing to Abbie.

'Wha … whi … whe …?' said Abbie, trying to work out what to ask first.

'Pardon?' said Perdita, and cartwheeled across the lawn.

Abbie found her voice. 'What *is* this thing?'

'I told you. The Gobbleweb. Rescues spiders with mini-mum stress.'

'Did your dad invent it?'

Perdita looked at Abbie as if she'd just asked how many toes a three-toed sloth has. 'Of course. Very Odd Jobs need Very Odd Tools. You can't *buy* them.'

'That is *so* cool,' said Abbie. 'Do you think I'd be able to interview him?'

Perdita cartwheeled back over the lawn. 'I doubt it. He's very shy. Why do you want to?'

Abbie sighed and sat down on the grass. 'It's just – well, I want to be a journalist you see. And I'm looking for –'

'Journalist?' Perdita sat down next to her. 'Does that mean you're a digging about, snooping around sort of person?' Her oil-dark eyes bored into Abbie's.

'I – I s'pose so,' said Abbie doubtfully.

'Perfect!' Perdita jumped up. 'I've got just the job for you. When can you come over?'

'Well, I –'

'We need to get going straight away.' Perdita did a little skip. Then she knelt down and grasped Abbie's shoulders. 'Thank you, Abigail Hartley,' she said solemnly. 'You have no idea what this means to me.' She unzipped her gigantic grin.

It was a grin you couldn't refuse. Not that Abbie wanted to, when she thought about it. The summer holidays forked in her mind. To the left, six weeks of boredom and biscuit burglary with the Rotten Lot. To the right, fun, sniffery and sneakage with this exclamation mark of a girl.

They went back to the sitting-room. Squashy was stuffing her knickers into her handbag. Ollie had come in and Mr Platt was showing him how to work the Crookhook.

Dad watched it claw the air. 'So versatile,' he marvelled, 'reaching books from shelves, painting the ceiling …'

'… Picking your sister's nose,' said Ollie, trying to.

'Get off!' squealed Abbie. 'This is my brother,' she said, rubbing her nose, 'Stink Bug.' She glared at him. Ollie burst into tears and howled off upstairs.

'Abigail!' came Mum's voice. 'Here. Now.'

Abbie ignored it. 'Dad's useless,' she explained to Mr Platt. 'He can tell you how the Romans unblocked their drains but he can't unblock ours.'

'Good job I teach history not plumbing, then.' Dad's laugh sounded like a drain *was* unblocking. Mr Platt smiled politely and unscrewed the Crookhook.

'Could Abigail come over to our house tomorrow, Mr Hartley?' asked Perdita.

'Well …' Dad pulled his beard.

'Please Dad,' said Abbie. 'I haven't been anywhere this hols.'

'I don't see why not.' Dad did the thumbs up at Mr Platt. 'Hunky dory by me, if it's hunky dory by you.'

Abbie winced. If being a plonker was an art, then Dad was Picasso.

'Of c-course.' Mr Platt rubbed a tooth with his finger. 'Though I'm not sure *house* is q-quite the word.' He finished packing while Perdita wrote out directions.

Abbie waved the green van off. Inventors, investigations and a not-quite house? The summer was looking up.

***

Back at the Platts' home, Matt unlocked the door of his workshop.

'What are you working on, Dad?' asked Perdita, trying to follow him in.

He pushed the door against her. 'Oh – oh nothing much. Why don't you go and get some lunch, darling?'

She frowned. 'Are you OK?'

'Yes. Yes of c-course.' Matt kissed her forehead. 'See you later.'

He locked the door behind her. Then he picked his way through a mess of boxes and books, tools and test tubes. He sat down at his desk and stared at the clump of white hair in front of him. How many strands should he mix in this time?

Matt rubbed his teeth miserably. Why was he doing this? Coriander had begged him not to. But didn't she see where it could lead? To her dream – building this place into a world centre of wonders! Hadn't she said there was nothing she wanted more? He put his head in his hands. There was nothing *he* wanted more than to see her again.

***

In her little room Coriander finished brushing Winnie's hair. She'd do anything to be back brushing Perdita's. She sighed. Winnie snuggled up to her.

Coriander kissed her forehead. 'Now then, Win,' she said briskly, 'how about some lunch?'

3

Missing

'Don't ask for biscuits,' said Mum the next afternoon. 'And you could've brushed your hair.' She turned left off the main road into a twisty lane.

'OK Mum, sorry Mum,' said Abbie, messing her milky coffee curls even more.

'And for goodness sake, take your wellies off inside.' They thought the Platts must live on a farm because Perdita's directions said park by a gate into a field.

They reached the gate. They thought again.

There was the field all right, muddy from last night's rain. It was dotted with dark green bushes. But it looked nothing like a farm. The bushes were squat and trimmed into strange shapes. *What's that called again*, thought Abbie. *Tapiry? Toppery? Topiary – that's it.* She grinned as she remembered one of her favourite car games: pointing out a heart or cockerel-shaped bush just in time for Ollie to miss it.

But there were no hearts or cockerels here. Only balls on stems. Some balls had a dangly triangle each side. Others were smooth on top with little tufts at the side. And others were large balls with small balls on top – like fat-bottomed number eights, or Big-Bum Beryl, Abbie's music teacher.

In the middle of the field stood a round tower. The bricks were fleshy pink. At the bottom of the tower was an arched wooden door. Above the door, in a vertical line, rose four round barred windows. The roof was rusty red thatch. It brushed the top window like a fringe. Two columns of interwoven thatch, also rusty red, hung down, one each side of the tower. And tied round the bottom of each column was a huge, yellow … *ribbon*. As if – well, as if the tower had plaits!

Abbie gasped. That was it. Hairstyles. Not just the tower, the bushes too. Those balls on stems were like heads on necks. The dangly triangles were bunches. The tufty bushes were balding heads. And the big-bottomed number eights were heads with buns.

Mum switched the engine off. Her mouth opened, closed and opened again.

'Cooo-*wul*,' breathed Abbie. She fingered the tape recorder in the right-hand pocket of her jacket.

The door in the tower opened. Perdita appeared, waving madly. She half bounced, half flew towards them like a great daddy longlegs. Her plaits danced, her eyes danced, even her *teeth* danced. She was wearing a pair of hairy trousers which looked like they'd been hacked from the hide of some mountain beast.

24

'You can't go in there!' hissed Mum from the side of her mouth.

'Please,' Abbie whispered, 'I'll be fine.'

'We don't *know* them. That girl looks bonkers.'

Of course she's bonkers, thought Abbie. What she said, though, was, 'Perdita's lovely. She didn't laugh at Grandma.' That was a first among Abbie's friends. Mum raised an eyebrow.

'And Dad really liked Mr Platt.'

Perdita was climbing over the gate with a grin wider than her face. Abbie played her best card. 'We can't leave now. What would it *look* like?'

As usual, that did the trick. 'Then let me come in with you,' sighed Mum.

You just dare, thought Abbie. What she said was, 'Your shoes. They'll be ruined.'

Mum glanced from her pearly pumps to the muddy field. 'Well, I don't know. You *must* take my phone then. Ring the minute you've had enough.' Abbie put the phone in her left pocket, on top of the packet of Jammy Dodgers she'd stolen from the snack cupboard.

'I must be mad,' muttered Mum. 'The Bellinghams don't let Tallulah post a *letter* on her own – and she's *twelve*.'

Perdita's grin barged through the car window. 'Helloo there!'

'Aargh!' Mum jerked backwards in her seat. Then she collected her face and switched on a smile. 'You must be Perdita.' She put her hand to her head and combed through Bob with her fingers. 'Nice to meet you, dear.'

'Bye Mum,' said Abbie firmly. 'See you at five.' She jumped out and slammed the door. Perdita vaulted back over the gate into the field. Abbie clambered after her and waved. Mum mouthed something bossy and drove off.

'Do you like my designs?' asked Perdita, waving towards the bushes.

'Brilliant,' said Abbie. 'You're a great gardener.'

Perdita laughed. 'Hairdresser, you mean. The bushes are just for practice. If you can style yew, you can style anything.'

They followed a path that wove between the bushes to the tower. When they reached the front door Perdita stepped out of her hairy trousers, revealing tatty jeans underneath. She hung the outer pair on a hook by the door.

'Must fix that,' she murmured, peering at a hole in the right knee. Then she brushed bits of brown hair off her jeans. 'Yak,' she explained. 'Gets everywhere.'

Abbie stared up at the thatched plaits. 'What *is* this place?' she asked.

'Oh, right. I forgot to introduce you.' Perdita cleared her throat. 'Welcome,' she said grandly, 'to The Platt Institute of Hirsute Pursuits.' She stood up and threw her arms out, smacking Abbie in the face. 'Oops, sorry.'

'The *what*?' said Abbie, rubbing her nose.

'OK,' Perdita muttered, 'just call it The Museum of Hair. Come on.'

Abbie followed her through the front door. When her eyes had adjusted to the gloom, she made out a circular room with a stone floor. It was empty apart from a fat pillar in the middle, which rose to the ceiling. There was an archway in its side.

Perdita had already gone through. 'This way,' she called.

Abbie followed, shivering in the damp air. Inside the hollow pillar was a spiral staircase that rose up the centre of the tower. She panted up the stone steps after Perdita, putting out a hand to steady herself against the wall. Her fingers touched moss. The cool air smelt sweet and vaguely familiar: a cross between strawberry jelly and bathroom cleaner.

Abbie reached a circular landing. Perdita was waiting by a door in the pillar wall. At the top of the door hung a crooked metal sign.

Perdita turned the handle and beckoned her in. The sweet smell rushed up Abbie's nose, making her gag. Hairspray – that was it – like the stuff Mum squirted over Bob every morning. Abbie stopped in the doorway and looked round.

At first glance the room was full of people.

At second glance they were standing or sitting, still as statues.

At third glance they *were* statues – or rather tailors' dummies in costumes.

At fourth glance the one on the left looked strangely familiar.

At fifth glance –

'Hi Robin,' said Perdita.

And there he was. Robin Hood. Well, a model of him, large as life and clothed in faded green. He looked very sorry for himself. His tunic was ripped. His breeches were frayed. A longbow sagged from his right shoulder, a quiverful of arrows from his left. His feather cap was dusty and his painted eyes lopsided.

But his hair! It gushed from his fibreglass chin, perky and red. It crawled across his brows like two hairy caterpillars. And it sat beneath his hat, glossy and smug.

'How are you today, Rob?' asked Perdita, patting his hand. 'Has Dad got round to fixing you?' She pressed a button on his thumb. His left hand unhooked the bow from his shoulder. His right hand plucked an arrow from the quiver. He aimed at the ceiling. The string drew back. Then the bow and arrow nosedived and Robin shot himself in the foot.

Perdita sighed and pulled the arrow out. 'Nope,' she muttered. 'Let's try Einstein.' She went over to the next model: an old man standing by a desk. He held a piece of chalk in his right hand. Behind him was a blackboard. His jacket and trousers were dusty with chalk. But his hair – again it looked almost alive. It cuddled his lip in a snowy moustache. It whizzed and fizzed and sprang from his head in wild white wires.

'Pull that lever on the desk,' said Perdita.

'Whoooaaauuh?' said Abbie, which would have been a

reasonable noise for someone yanking a handle to make, but was actually the sound of all her questions crashing out of her mouth at once.

She pulled the lever. Einstein turned to the board and began to scribble with the chalk.

Abbie read what he'd written. *Ee, it's a messy square.* 'I – I thought it was supposed to be E = MC squared.'

'It is,' sighed Perdita. 'Dad has some great ideas. But they don't always quite work.' She sat down on the floor and hugged her knees.

'What *is* this place?' whispered Abbie, crouching next to her. 'And why does the hair look so real?'

'Because it *is.*'

Abbie stared at Perdita. She didn't have the sort of face that pulled legs. But what on earth …?

Perdita jumped up. 'Come and see for yourself.' She ran over to a model of a lady in a white robe. The lady was sitting by a small paddling pool that was half full of water. Toy boats huddled against the side furthest away from her. 'Helen of Troy,' said Perdita. She took a handful of the lady's hair. It was dazzling. It poured down her back like golden syrup. Fat lashes curled from her painted blue eyes. Golden eyebrows arched on her forehead.

Helen of Troy, thought Abbie, *the face that launched a thousand ships*. Wouldn't Dad love this! He was always banging on about that ancient Greek king who'd led a fleet of a thousand ships to Troy to rescue his beautiful wife Helen. And at the end of the story Mum always asked the same thing: would Dad launch a thousand ships if she was kidnapped? And Dad always assured her, '*Ten* thousand, my angel.'

'Go on,' said Perdita, 'feel it.'

Abbie came up to Helen and reached out a trembling hand. The hair felt as silky and cool as butter.

'Now press her nose,' said Perdita.

Abbie pressed. The boats in the paddling pool shot into the air. They soared towards Helen, then over her head, and crashed into the wall behind her.

Perdita tutted. 'Oh dear. The face that launched a thousand aeroplanes.' She went over to the wall and started picking up the boats. Then she hurled them at the wall. 'Dad's giving up!' she cried. A tear splashed onto the floor.

Abbie came over. She patted Perdita on the arm and said the most comforting words she could think of. 'Jammy Dodger?'

Perdita grinned through her tears. 'Thanks.' They sat on the floor. Perdita took a sniffly bite. Crumbs sprayed everywhere. 'He's giving up,' she went on, 'because he thinks she won't come back.'

'Who won't?' asked Abbie.

'My mum. She's gone. Disappeared. Ten weeks, four days and –' Perdita counted on her fingers – 'eight hours ago. We got up one morning and there she wasn't.'

The first question that flashed across Abbie's mind was *who made your breakfast then?* Wisely she asked the second. 'Did you call the police?'

31

'Not straight away. Mum had been called to Spain urgently. That was no big deal. Mum's a world expert on hair, you see, and she often has to –' Perdita sniffed – '*had* to, leave at short notice. To check out interesting finds.'

'Like what?' asked Abbie.

'A strand of Cleopatra's eyebrow, a hair from Shakespeare's moustache, that sort of thing.'

'But what's interesting about a few old hairs?'

'If they turn out to be real, Mum brings –' Perdita sniffed again – '*brought* them, back to the museum. Then Dad dipped them into this mixture he invented to make the hairs grow.'

'What do you mean "grow"?' asked Abbie, who had a funny feeling she knew exactly what Perdita meant. She was right.

'Get longer, sprout, thicken,' said Perdita. 'All the things hair does.'

Abbie stared at her, blank as a blanket.

'Look,' said Perdita, pointing to a model dressed in pirate clothes. 'Take Blackbeard. Mum collected a tiny tangle of his beard. Then Dad dipped it in the mixture, and hey presto.' The model's painted brown eyes glared at Abbie between furious eyebrows and a coal-black beard. Abbie swallowed. This was so crazy you couldn't make it up.

Perdita took a photo out of her pocket. 'There's Mum in Israel,' she said, handing it to Abbie. 'She's just dug up the end of Abraham's beard.' A big lady with a round face was beaming under a tree. She wore a blue tent of a dress.

One arm was raised high above her head. Hanging from her finger and thumb was a cloud of white hair.

But it was the *lady's* hair that made Abbie squeal. 'Red plaits with yellow ribbons – she looks like this tower!'

'Other way round,' said Perdita. 'The museum was her idea, so Dad and I thatched the tower to look like *her*. We did it a few months before she left.'

Abbie thought for a minute. 'That morning … how do you know your mum had gone to Spain if she'd left by the time you woke up? Did she leave a note or something?'

'No. Mum had told my aunt – she lives here too with my uncle, you see. Mum woke Auntie Mell to say there'd been this phone call from an archaeologist. He was digging in the ruins of a castle near Barcelona. And he found a golden hair comb with a few strands of black hair. He thought they might belong to Wilfred the Hairy, Count of Barcelona, who lived more than a thousand years ago. So Mum flew over there to check.'

'Why didn't she wake you?'

'She told Auntie Mell not to disturb me, she'd be back that night.' Perdita shook her head. Her plaits whacked her cheeks. 'But there's more to it than that. I heard Mum and Dad arguing the night before. And they *never* argue –' Perdita sniffed her sniffliest sniff yet – 'I mean argued. Dad still won't tell me what it was about.' She wiped her nose with a plait. 'And we haven't heard from Mum since.'

'Not even a phone call?'

'No calls, no letters. I try her mobile phone every day,

but it just says the number's not available. The police have searched all over, here and in Spain. And now they say she might be …' Perdita's teeth ploughed her chin. 'But I know she isn't.'

Abbie wasn't at all sure how someone could sound so sure about something that didn't sound so sure at all. What she said, though, was, 'Sure.'

'Even my aunt and uncle are beginning to lose hope. They say I've got to start facing reality.' Perdita tugged her front plaits fiercely. 'But I am! I know Mum's still out there. And I know she still loves us.'

Abbie squeezed Perdita's arm. 'I wish I could help you.'

Perdita slotted a Jammy Dodger into her mouth like a giant coin. 'You can. Find her.'

If you'd poured petrol over Abbie's knickers and lit a match she couldn't have jumped up faster. '*What?!*'

Perdita brushed crumbs from her mouth. 'You're a journalist. There's your story.'

If you'd squashed a tomato on Abbie's face and squirted ketchup on top she couldn't have gone redder. 'No! I mean how can I – I mean *what* can I – ?'

'Think about it,' said Perdita, standing up. 'Now come and see Henry the Eighth.'

She ran over to a barrel-shaped model of a man. He wore a bejewelled tunic and stood with his legs wide apart. A red beard rimmed his chin and fat cheeks. On his head sat a furry pancake of a hat. His right hand grasped his hip. His left hand clutched an axe.

Perdita pushed the axe and jumped back. The king's arm lifted. The axe swung above the hat. 'Off with her head,' growled a voice deep within his fibre glass chest. 'Off with her head. Off wiith herrrr heauu …' The voice wilted.

'Battery dead,' muttered Perdita. 'Oh dearie me. How about you, Sam?'

Next to the king towered a huge figure. His head was bent and his palms pressed against two plaster pillars either side. He was covered from head to toe in dark brown hair. It glowed and flowed. It glistened and gleamed. It poured onto the floor like melted chocolate. It sprouted from his chest, thick as a doormat. It swamped his face in beard.

'Samson?' gasped Abbie. That bruiser from the Bible whose strength lay in his hair? That really took the biscuit. She took a biscuit.

'Remember how he pushed down pillars with his bare hands and killed loads of Philistines? Watch.' Perdita stamped on the model's foot. His right hand, pressing against its pillar, cracked and fell off.

'Oh for goodness sake!' shouted Perdita. She looked at Abbie. They burst out laughing.

'Hang on.' Abbie wiped her eyes. The Mexican Hat Dance was blaring from her pocket. She fished out the phone.

'Hi darling,' came Mum's too-bright voice. 'Slight emergency. Dad needs the car. See you at the gate. Bye.'

'Mum, it's not even –'

But Mum had rung off. Abbie stuck out her tongue at the phone. 'Can you believe it? I've got to go.'

She put the phone back in her pocket and felt the edge of the tape recorder. Some journalist. She'd forgotten to switch it on.

'Ring me,' said Perdita, leading the way to the door.

Abbie turned for one last look at the room. Wonky eyes gazed out beneath whizzy hairstyles. As she turned away something grey streaked across the floor.

'Yeeuggh,' Abbie gasped, 'a rat!' She shot after Perdita.

***

On the floor above Hairstory, Matt was peering through a magnifying glass. He'd just squeezed three drops of liquid from a pipette onto a woodlouse. The creature was scuttling round his desk. Matt sighed. Poor thing. Better take it back to its family.

Hang on a mo. Its back was sprouting tiny white hairs!

Matt sighed again. So what? A hairy back didn't mean the mixture had worked. How on earth could you *tell* with a woodlouse? Oh, this was getting nowhere.

Matt threw the magnifying glass down. He grabbed the end of his left plait and yanked off the elastic band. He did the same with his right plait, then the one at the back. There. He ran his fingers through his hair. It flopped onto his shoulders, greasy and sad. He'd plait it again when Coriander came back … or rather *if*.

***

Coriander pulled her two front plaits out of Minnie's hands. 'Leave them alone, Min,' she laughed. 'They're all I've got left of my family. This plait for Matt, this one for Perdita and the one at the back for me. They keep my hopes up.'

Minnie tugged her hand.

'All right dear,' said Coriander, 'I'll play with you. After I've finished my letter. And please don't wee on it, like you did on the last one.'

4

Rotten Lot

'Are you OK darling? I was so worried.' Mum turned round in the front seat with her stick-on smile.

Abbie scowled from the back. 'Course I am. Why does Dad need the car?'

'He doesn't.' Mum took a hand off the steering wheel to smooth Bob. 'I just wasn't happy. That place is so –' she gave a little shudder – 'weird.'

'What?!' Abbie exploded. 'You made it up, just so you could collect me early? How *could* you?'

'Abigail,' said Mum, meeting her glare in the rear view mirror, 'we don't *know* these people. It was for your own good.'

'*Your* own good you mean,' Abbie muttered. 'I was having the best time ever. Their house is amazing. You wouldn't believe it.'

'Let me guess,' said Mum. 'Persian rugs. Oak kitchen like the Bellinghams?'

Abbie prayed for peace on earth and goodwill to all parents. 'I didn't get to *see* the kitchen, thanks to you. The whole place is a mess. I loved it. You'd hate it.'

Mum ignored the insult. 'What's Mrs Platt like? My kind of person?'

Abbie doubted that very much. 'How do I know?' She saw her chance for a neat little lie. 'I was just about to go upstairs and meet her when you phoned. Perdita was so upset I had to go. She's *really* nice.'

'Please darling,' said Mum, 'I only did it to protect you. Look, maybe Perdita could come over to us next time.'

And see what I have to put up with? thought Abbie. *Why not?* 'Tomorrow?' she asked.

'Sure.' Mum unlocked the front door. The smell of tuna fish and orange slid up Abbie's nostrils. Oh no. Dad must be doing dinner.

He came out of the kitchen in a frilly white apron. 'Hi Abbie. Everything OK?' He waved a wooden spoon. 'Mum was a bit concerned.'

'I know,' Abbie growled. 'It was brilliant, Dad. They live in this museum. It's full of hair. Mum ruined it.'

'Hair?'

Abbie sighed. 'I mean hair*styles*. From history.'

'A costume museum. How fascinating. Wigs and dresses and all that?'

Abbie nodded. Why explain more? It would only freak Mum out and ruin any chance of visiting again. 'Yep. Beards and buns and –'

'Buns!' echoed Squashy, coming in through the front door. She smacked her palm against her head. Her wig slipped down her forehead. 'Knew I'd forgotten somethin'.' She did a U-turn. Her shopping-bag-on-wheels ran over Abbie's foot.

'Ow!' muttered Abbie. 'Silly old –'

'Abigail!' said Mum, raising her eyebrows. 'You know Grandma can't see well without her glasses.'

'Thanks for the sympathy.' Abbie made a show of rubbing her foot, which didn't hurt at all.

'Don't be long, Mother,' Dad called as Grandma shuffled out of the front door. 'Dinner's in half an hour.'

If you could call it that. It looked like one of Mum's face packs, a brown and orange paste smeared on tortilla wraps.

'I've called it fish 'n' fruity funbites,' announced Dad. 'Rolls off the tongue, doesn't it?'

That's what I'm worried about, thought Abbie.

'The recipe says chicken,' said Dad, 'but I thought tuna would give more of a kick.'

'Fish can't kick,' said Ollie, sitting down next to Abbie. 'They haven't got legs.' He shrieked with laughter.

'But I have,' she said, kicking his ankle. He howled.

'Abigail!' cried Mum.

'Stop that!' barked Dad.

'Sorry,' mumbled Abbie. 'Just a joke.'

'You're tellin' me,' said Squashy, appearing in the doorway and eyeing the table. 'Joke of a dinner.'

'Please try it, Mother,' said Dad.

Grandma glared at him and sat down – *ohno* – opposite Abbie. 'Pass the salt.' She shook the pot until her plate gleamed like a frosty morning. Then she grabbed the wrap in her fist and stuffed it into her mouth. The food hurtled round her open jaws like cement in a mixer. Every few bites her top teeth came unstuck. She half sucked, half shoved them back up with her thumb. Abbie's jaw dropped in wonder at the sight.

'Abigail,' said Mum, 'don't eat with your mouth open.'

The cheek. The unbe*liev*able cheek. 'But look at Gra–'

'Abigail, I said close your mouth.'

'You mean like this, Mummy?' said Ollie, pressing his lips together and chewing prettily.

'Exactly, darling. You see, Ollie can do it. And he's only five.'

'So,' said Dad hurriedly, 'tell us more about this museum, Abbie.'

She stared at her plate. 'I told you.'

'Mum said it's the most amazing building.'

'Mmm.'

'I thought you were very brave to go in, darling,' said Mum in her sorry-without-actually-saying-sorry voice. 'The whole place gave me the creeps.'

They ate in silence – not counting Squashy's slurping and slapping – until Dad said, 'Who's for seconds?'

'Me,' said Abbie, out of hunger rather than appreciation.

Mum frowned. 'Haven't you had enough, darling? I've noticed you're getting a bit of a tum.'

That was it. 'Leave me alone!' Abbie shoved her chair back. She ran out of the kitchen, upstairs and into her bedroom. She slammed the door and hurled herself onto the bed.

'Rotten,' she snarled, 'Lot.' She kicked a cushion across the floor. She chewed a mouthful of duvet. She punched the pillow that Mum had made when she was a baby. She grabbed the photo of the family on the beach in Cornwall. 'Rotten Lot!' she shouted, and threw it across the room.

Abbie stuck out her tongue at the photo. Then she went over, picked it up and sat on the edge of her bed. She blocked out Mum with her thumb. Why couldn't *she* disappear instead of Mrs Platt? Perdita's mum sounded brilliant. *She* wouldn't collect Perdita early from friends with some stupid lie. *She* wouldn't stop her having second helpings. *She* wouldn't goo over maggoty little brothers.

There was a knock at the door. Abbie dropped the photo onto the floor and pulled the duvet round her ears.

'Can I come in?' said Dad, who already had. 'I'm sorry you're upset, darling.'

'Mum's always on at me. She tells me off for everything. She hates me.'

'Course she doesn't. She loves you more than anything. She's just trying to help.'

'By picking me up early when I'm having the best time ever?'

'She was worried about you.'

'By telling me off when Grandma's manners are ten times worse?'

'You're our daughter. Grandma isn't,' said Dad.

'Wow, I'd never noticed,' said Abbie sarcastically. 'And Mum always makes a fuss when I want seconds.'

'Join the club.' Dad sat down on the bed and patted his stomach. 'I guess she doesn't understand our big bones.'

Abbie nodded. Mum had the bones of a stunted sparrow and an appetite to match. Then she scowled again. 'Why does she always take Ollie's side? It's like he's this delicate little cutie pie.'

Dad sighed. 'He's just younger than you, darling. And you can be a bit – rough.'

'So he gets away with everything. Not fair!'

'I'm sorry,' said Dad. 'We try to be fair. But you and Ollie – well, your needs are different. And I guess we all get it wrong sometimes.' He put his arm round her. She glared at the ground. 'Now,' he said brightly, 'how about some Banoffee pie? A Dad special.'

Which turned out to be banana with coffee instead of toffee. 'Gives more of a kick,' said Dad.

As Abbie aimed for Ollie's

ankle again, a happy thought danced across her mind. Of course!

Her foot froze. She took her pudding, said thank you, chewed politely, said thank you again, didn't ask for seconds and offered to wash up.

'How kind of you, darling. Don't worry, I'll do it,' said Mum in her sorry-again-without-saying-it voice.

'Can I phone Perdita then?' asked Abbie. 'You said I could invite her tomorrow.'

'Go ahead.'

Abbie ran up to her room with Mum's cell phone and closed the door.

The phone rang for ages. Then a soft singsong voice said, 'Helloo?'

'Um, may I speak to Perdita?' asked Abbie.

'Certainly. Who is it, please?'

'Abbie Hartley.'

'Oh, of *course*. This is her aunt speaking. Perdie's told me all about you. So sorry to miss you. *Do* come again soon. Here she is. Toodleoo.'

Perdita sounded breathless. 'I had to run up two flights.'

'I was wondering,' said Abbie. 'Could you come over tomorrow afternoon?'

There was a pause. Then, 'Thank you,' said Perdita. 'I just knew you would.'

'Would what?' gasped Abbie. 'How d'you – ?'

'I'll be there at two. Bye.'

Abbie switched on her tape recorder. 'FRIEND IN

NEED,' she told the microphone. 'In a fantastic show of friendship, plucky Abigail Hartley has promised to help her pal Perdita to find her long-lost mother.' Abbie pressed the Pause button. How long did someone have to be lost to be long-lost? Oh never mind. She pressed Play again. 'When asked what gave her the guts for such a mission, our heroic Abigail said, "It's all thanks to the Rotten Lot. I can't wait to get away from them."'

***

Sitting at his desk, Matt breathed out with relief. Thank goodness that phone call was for Perdita. It would keep her out of the way for a bit. It was awful having to be so secretive: locking her out, avoiding her questions. But until these experiments worked – until he could make everything right – Perdita mustn't know. Like Coriander, she'd never approve. He was playing with fire.

Not that any sparks were flying yet. Matt sighed. Very carefully he picked up the centipede on his desk with a pair of tweezers. He dipped the creature into his latest potion. 'Sorry, poppet,' he whispered, 'but it's all for the best.' He placed the centipede back on his desk and peered through his magnifying glass. Dark brown hairs were sprouting from its head.

'Useless!' exclaimed Matt, hitting his forehead. Even if the mixture *had* made the centipede's legs stronger so that it could crawl faster, those new hairs would just weigh the creature down. So the overall effect would be – zilch.

Matt burst into tears. Oh, for a shoulder to cry on. A comforting, cuddly Coriander shoulder.

***

Coriander tapped Vinnie on the shoulder. 'Wakey wakey,' she cooed. 'Bath time.' Vinnie opened a lazy eye.

Winnie was already in the tub pushing round a plastic duck with her finger. Vinnie yawned and clambered in with her.

'You too, Minnie,' called Coriander. 'It's lovely and warm.' Minnie cowered in the corner.

'All right,' said Coriander. 'I'll put in extra bubble bath, just for you.' She emptied half the bottle of Matey into the water. Minnie turned her back on Coriander.

Coriander began to hum: a low, sweet tune she used to sing when Perdita was little. Slowly Minnie turned round. Slowly she came towards the tub. And slowly she climbed in.

5

Dandruff

The next day at two o'clock sharp Perdita was at the door. She was clutching a plastic ice cream box. The battered green van was already driving away. 'Dad's off to charm a chimney,' she explained.

Abbie didn't ask.

Perdita bounded past her, through the hall, and into the kitchen. 'Hi Mrs Hartley.'

'Hello dear.' Mum was peeling carrots.

Perdita held out the ice cream box. 'I baked these for you.'

Mum wiped her not-at-all-messy hands and took the box. 'How kind,' she said, in a voice that you'd never guess had been banging on about That Weird Girl all morning. She opened the lid. 'Biscuits. They smell delicious. We'll have some later.'

Ollie came in through the back door.

'Hello again,' said Perdita, letting loose more grin.

'You look like a piano,' he said.

'Ollie!' said Mum.

'Louse,' said Abbie.

But Perdita was laughing. 'Upright or grand?'

'Come on,' said Abbie, 'let's go outside.' She slammed the back door behind them.

Ollie squashed his face against the glass. He looked like one of those little dogs that old ladies dress in coats. 'Can I come?' he mouthed.

Abbie shook her head. But Perdita opened the back door again and said, 'Give us fifteen minutes. Then I'll play catch with you.'

Ollie's eyes widened. 'Promise?'

'Promise.'

Ollie did a happy hop and went away.

'What d'you say that for?' said Abbie. 'I thought you'd come to see *me*.'

Perdita did a handstand on the patio. 'I haven't got a brother. I'd love to play with him.' She ran across the lawn. On the far side she stopped. 'This hedge looks like it's been dragged through a hedge,' she said, peering at a mess of twigs and weed-choked stems. 'Shall I trim it for you? I could do a pony tail.'

Abbie came over. 'I'm not sure what Mum would think about that.' Or, to be more precise, what Mum would think the *neighbours* would think. 'She's not really into – um – plant art. Let's go and sit in the treehouse. We can talk in private there.'

On the other side of the hedge was another smaller lawn. In the far corner stood a tree. A jumble of planks clung to its lower branches. At the foot of the tree stood an old rabbit hutch.

Perdita bent down and peered through the grille. 'Where's the rabbit?'

Abbie kicked the hutch. 'We haven't got one. This was here when we moved in. And Dad's never bothered to get rid of it. So it just sits there reminding me that we aren't allowed pets.'

'Why not?' said Perdita, stroking the hutch as if it *was* a rabbit.

'Mum says she'd end up cleaning it out – and she's had enough poo for one lifetime from me and Ollie. And Dad says it's too much hassle to get bunnysitters every time we go on holiday.'

'Oh well. Brothers are better than pets,' said Perdita. She hoisted herself into the tree.

'My brother *is* a pet,' said Abbie. 'Teacher's pet. Mother's pet. Pet worm if you ask me.'

Perdita sat down cross-legged on a rickety plank. She reached out a hand to help Abbie up. The plank sagged. 'Did your dad make this treehouse?' she asked.

'Can't you tell?' said Abbie.

'Maybe my dad could fix it.'

'Your dad's so cool,' said Abbie.

'Wait till you meet my mum,' said Perdita. 'When shall we go?'

'Go where?'

'To Spain. To find her. All we need is the money for air fares. Plus a bit extra for emergencies.'

'Hang on,' said Abbie. 'I never said I was going to Spain!'

Perdita threw up her hands. 'Well how else are we going to find her?'

Beyond escaping the Rotten Lot, Abbie hadn't really thought up a plan. But Perdita was right. Of course they'd have to go. And Spain did sound rather fun – all those tortillas and toreadors.

'Look,' said Perdita. She shoved a hand into her pocket. Out came three crumpled five pound notes and a handful of coins. 'I've got £22.75. I reckon we need about £30 more. You can get some really cheap flights these days.'

Abbie had £3.32 in her piggy bank. The rest of her pocket money went on weekly essentials like Crunchie bars. 'How are we going to make £30?'

'Easy.' Perdita jumped up. The plank creaked like Grandma on the loo. 'There's always loads of work to do round the museum. I asked Dad if he'd start paying me. So now he gives me £2 for every job. It adds up. And if you help out, he'll pay you too. That's seven and a half jobs each.'

'Why not just ask him for the air fare?'

Perdita snorted. 'Why not ask a pig for bacon? Dad would *never* let me go. This is the first time I've been allowed to go anywhere on my own since Mum left. It's like Dad's scared I'll disappear too.'

Abbie rubbed her fingers along the plank, thinking hard. 'So how will he feel if you do disappear? To Spain, I mean.'

Perdita draped herself over a branch. 'Mmm. That *is* a worry.'

'Unless – ow!' Abbie pulled a splinter from her finger. 'Unless *I* go. Alone.'

Perdita swung down to Abbie, nearly kicking her out of the tree. She shoved her face up close. 'But what about *your* family? How would *they* feel if *you* disappeared?'

Hmm, thought Abbie, *now let me see. Grandma wouldn't notice, Ollie wouldn't care, Dad would look up famous disappearances in history and Mum would have a facial to cheer herself up.* What she said was, 'No problem – I can handle them. *And* it would mean only one air fare.'

'I s'pose so,' said Perdita, sounding a little doubtful. Well, as doubtful as a girl with big teeth and even bigger plans can sound.

Ollie waved from the lawn.

'Playtime,' said Perdita. She jumped down from the treehouse.

'By the way,' whispered Abbie, as they went over, 'don't tell Mum about the museum. It's way off her weird scale. If she hears it's got real hair she'll never let me come again.'

'Then I'd better not tell her what's in those biscuits I brought,' murmured Perdita.

'What *is* in them?'

'Dandruff.'

Abbie gave a gasping gurgle; or was it a gurgling gasp?

'Don't worry,' said Perdita reassuringly, 'just think of it as brain peel. Full of vitamins.' She crept up to Ollie. 'I'm coming to *get* you!' Ollie shrieked as she grabbed him in a bear hug. Then he wriggled free and dashed off round the lawn. Perdita ran after him, huffing and puffing in pretend exhaustion.

Abbie watched them. Her stomach went tight. Why hadn't Ollie asked *her* to play? She joined in the chase.

'Two against one,' yelled Ollie. 'Noffair!'

'Suit yourself,' she snapped and humphed down on the patio.

Mum knocked on the kitchen window. 'Yoo hoo,' she called. 'Anyone for biscuits?'

They trooped inside. Ollie and Perdita were panting and giggling. 'You're too quick for me,' said Perdita, wagging her finger at him.

'And I'm only five,' he said proudly. He sat next to her at the table.

Grandma appeared at the door. It usually annoyed Abbie the way Squashy shared her gift for sniffing out snacks: partly because it was a reminder that they were related, and partly because Abbie hated sharing snacks. Not this time though. For once she was delighted to watch Grandma, and everyone else, grab a biscuit.

'Coconut!' said Mum, examining the little white flakes. 'My favourite. You must give me the recipe, dear.'

'It's actually da–' said Perdita. Abbie kicked her under the table '… Dad's secret. But I can make you some more.'

'You have such an interesting house.' Mum took another biscuit.

Mum, seconds? Blimey, thought Abbie, *call the doctor.*

'I hear it's a museum for hair,' said Mum, nibbling delicately.

'Just a few wigs,' said Perdita casually. It was my mum's idea. She dis–' Abbie kicked her ankle again '… designed the whole place. She's a hairdresser.'

'How lovely. I've often fancied hairdressing,' said Mum, stroking Bob. 'I'd love to meet her.'

'Definitely,' said Perdita definitely.

''Airdressin'?' said Grandma. 'Waste of time if you ask me. Snippin' and stylin', potions and lotions – it all falls out in the end. And then you 'ave to buy one of *these* itchy devils.' She scratched her wig. It slipped over her left ear.

Abbie closed her eyes. Couldn't Squashy once – just once – behave herself in front of visitors?

But Perdita was nodding in sympathy. 'You need a better wig. There are some great ones around now.'

Squashy jiggled her false teeth impatiently. 'And where would I find one of those, young lady?'

'Perdita was only trying to help, Grandma,' said Abbie.

'It's OK,' said Perdita cheerfully. 'I'll see if we've got a spare one at the museum.'

'None of them fancy Mozart jobs, mind,' said Grandma.

'What a sweet girl you are,' Mum said, beaming at Perdita.

Abbie grinned. Never mind Mr Platt and his chimneys. Perdita was charming the pants off Mum. No worries about Abbie visiting again.

***

Matt put away the Soot Soothing Spray. 'That should c-calm your chimney down, Mrs Fugg,' he said. 'C-call me if you have any more problems.'

'Thank you Mr Platt. Me cough's better already. What do I owe you?'

Matt looked from Mrs Fugg's frayed slippers to the holes in her cardigan. 'Don't mention it,' he said. 'I'm glad I c-could help.'

'You're an angel,' she said, her baggy face crinkling with gratitude.

Matt got into the van and sighed. No wonder he earned so little from Very Odd Jobbing. Mustn't tell Perdita. She'd tick him off again for being too soft. And she'd be right. Money was getting very tight. Which was why his experiments *had* to succeed.

***

'Hold still, love. It'll hurt if you wriggle.' Coriander clipped Winnie's narrow fingernail. It reminded her of clipping Perdita's. A tear fell onto the nail scissors. Winnie kissed Coriander's hand.

'Thank you dear.' Coriander blew her nose and looked at her watch. Still four hours to go till her rounds. Till she could escape this stinky room and breathe fresh (well, fresh-ish) air again. Better go and wash the brushes and combs. Oh, and sharpen the hair scissors. Wasn't Silvio due for a trim? He'd get upset if it took too long.

And you really didn't want to upset Silvio.

6

Hoot

Dad insisted on taking Abbie the next day.

'Stone the crows,' he murmured, parking by the field. 'Pelt the puffins,' he gasped, catching sight of the hedges with hairstyles. 'Bomb the buzzards!' he cried, staring at the plaited pink tower.

He opened the car door. 'I'll just pop in with you, Abbs.' He was trying to sound all cool. 'Keen to see this hair business.'

'No!' squeaked Abbie. No way was Dad coming in. This was *her* adventure. 'The thing is,' she gabbled, 'Mr Platt's too busy. He hasn't got time to show you round.'

Dad's big face drooped as only big faces can. 'Just for a min? Maybe Perdita could give me a tour.'

'No.' Abbie shook her head till it hurt. 'She's busy too. Bye, Dad.' She clambered onto the gate.

'Oh, Mum said remember to eat with your mouth closed,' Dad shouted to her back.

Perdita was waiting at the front door. She seized Abbie's hand. 'Dad's given us a great job to do. He said he'll pay us £3 each! Come on.' She leapt up the stairs.

Abbie puffed after her. 'My mum thinks you're lovely,' she panted.

'I think she is too,' Perdita shouted down the stairs.

Abbie reached the first landing. Without waiting for her to get her breath back, Perdita hared up the next flight. Abbie joined her on the second landing. It was exactly like the first, except for the sign over the door.

'Hair Science,' she read. 'What's that?'

'It's where Dad does his inventing.' Perdita tried the door handle. 'Locked again,' she sighed. 'Ever since Mum left it's out of bounds. Never used to be. Up we go.' And she was off again.

Abbie staggered up to the next landing. They must have climbed nearly a hundred stairs. No wonder Perdita was so skinny.

The sign on the door said:

Rare Hair

'This was – *is* – Mum's favourite room,' said Perdita. Abbie got ready to gasp. The gasp died in her throat.

The room was dotted with glass cases and things on stands. Apart from a large empty cage on the left, it looked just like a normal museum, the sort that's full of ancient tools and bits of pottery, with draughty bathrooms and loo seats that make your bottom ping with cold. The sort that's duller than dust on dung.

Except –

On a stand in front of her sat a stuffed bird. It was the size of a goose. But instead of feathers it had shaggy white hair. Its beak was a hairy tube. At the front of the tube was a round flap, like a lid.

'What's that?' asked Abbie. The bird fixed Abbie with cold glass eyes, as if insulted that she'd had to ask.

'A Hairy Hoot,' said Perdita. 'From Greenland. They were hunted to extinction a hundred years ago.'

'Why?'

'People used their beaks as thermos flasks. The hair keeps the heat in – perfect for hot drinks. Mum found this one preserved in ice.'

Abbie didn't remember reading about Hairy Hoots in her book *Dodos and Other Dead Dudes*.

But before she could say so, Perdita grabbed her arm and led her to a glass case.

'Look at *this*, then.'

Abbie could see Perdita was waiting for a 'wow'. But it's hard to 'wow' at a piece of silver string pinned to a cushion. So instead she read out the label on the case. 'Single hair of the Bald Bobus (*Baldus bobissimus*).'

'It's the only one in captivity,' said Perdita proudly. 'Took Mum three years to collect it. Go on.'

'*The Bald Bobus,*' Abbie read, '*is a nocturnal mammal the size of a squirrel. It nests under the Yabooka tree in the Borneo jungle. It spends up to four hours a day polishing its single hair. The hair grows for six years. Then it is pushed out by the next emerging strand. The Bobus uses the moulted hair as a skipping rope. Lifespan: twenty-one years (three and a half hairs).*'

Abbie snorted. 'Oh come on! Never heard of it.'

'Few people have,' said Perdita, 'let alone *seen* it. But Mum did. Four years ago. It was gathering berries at night. She guessed, from the length of its hair, that it would fall out after two years, ten months and twelve days. So last year she went back to the same spot. And watch this.'

Fixed to the wall above the case was a TV and DVD player. Perdita stood on tiptoe and pressed Play. A crouching figure appeared in the foreground with its back turned. In the background was a nest made of twigs and leaves. For a minute nothing happened. Then a silver strand fell out of the nest. A tiny paw reached out to grab it. But the crouching figure reached forward and snatched it first. It put another silver thread into the creature's paw.

'That's Mum taking the hair. Did you see how she gave the Bobus a piece of silver string so it could still do its skipping?' asked Perdita.

Abbie's jaw reached for the floor.

Perdita slapped her on the back. 'Come on Fishface,' she laughed, 'I'll show you the fish.'

She led Abbie to the back of the room. Against the curving wall stood a fish tank. Abbie stared through the glass. Everything inside had hair: the plants, the stones on the bottom, even the fish. A tiny blue fish wove from left to right, trailing golden hairs twice its length. A sea horse bobbed towards Abbie with a bushy green mane and tail. An eel with a glittering red beard wriggled up the side of the tank. And a white crab with hairy legs scuttled across the bottom.

'The Hairyquarium,' said Perdita, handing Abbie a pot of fish food, 'Mum's pride and joy.'

Abbie sprinkled a few flakes onto the water. 'I – I had no idea there *were* such creatures. Why haven't I read about them?'

Perdita shrugged. 'Maybe no one's written about them. And even if they have, maybe no one believed them. Like this poor guy.' She skipped across the room to the empty cage on the left that Abbie had noticed before. What she hadn't noticed was the tangle of dark brown hair in one corner. Perdita reached through the bars and picked it up.

'Don't tell me,' said Abbie, holding up her hand as if to stop traffic. 'Nostril hair. From a yeti.'

Perdita squealed. 'How did you know?'

Abbie gulped. 'I was joking.'

'Well, you're spot on! Mum tweezed it from a sleeping yeti on Mount Everest. Dad's supposed to be growing it. Then we can have a yeti model in the cage covered in real hair.' Perdita sighed. '*If* he ever gets round to it.'

'Gets round to what, plumcake?'

The voice was soft and tinkly. Its owner, standing in the doorway, was elegant and thin. She wore a honey-coloured dress that matched her honey-coloured hair. She flowed across the room towards the girls.

'You must be Abbie. I'm Aunt Melliflua. We spoke on the phone.' She smiled. Her teeth were neat and tiny, like two rows of tic tacs. Her amber eyes were big and beautiful – or big and froglike – Abbie couldn't quite decide. They were certainly very shiny.

Aunt Melliflua took Abbie's hand. Her fingers were as cool as knitting needles.

'I'm so glad Perdie's made a friend. She gets quite lonely here, what with all the work round the museum and not going to school. Don't you sweetie?' She beamed at her niece.

'No school? You never told me. Lucky jammer!' said Abbie to Perdita. Aunt Melliflua's arched eyebrows arched

61

even more. 'Didn't she now? Really –' she wagged her finger at Perdita in mock annoyance – 'after all my hard work. I home school her, you see, sweetie,' she said to Abbie. 'Ever since her mother started all that travelling.' Aunt Melliflua shook her honey head. 'Such a terrible thing. Perdie's told you, has she?'

'Yes. I'm sorry.'

'My only sister.' Aunt Melliflua's shiny eyes went even shinier. 'But we have to carry on. I'm so glad Uncle Dirk and I are here to help.' She put her arm round Perdita.

'Me too Auntie.' Perdita snuggled against her.

Aunt Melliflua sighed. 'Anyway, sugar, just to remind you, dinner's at six.'

'Oh, sure.' Perdita looked at her watch. 'We'll just do this job for Dad then I'll come.'

'What *is* the job?' said Abbie.

'Mending a shrunken head.'

Aunt Melliflua's arm fell off Perdita's shoulder. 'Euggh! Not that thing! I can't understand why your mother brought it here. It's so …' she shuddered. 'Well, I'll leave you to it, then. Toodlepip. Lovely to meet you, sweetie.' Tickling the air in a little wave, she glided out the door.

And when Perdita showed her the shrunken head, Abbie felt like gliding out too.

***

Downstairs in Hair Science Matt stared at the ant. It scuttled round the matchbox in exactly the same way as *before* he'd dipped it into the mixture. How could you *tell* if it was brainier, for goodness sake? Give it a sum and a pen to write the answer? The poor little mite would be crushed in an instant.

Talking of writing – still no letter from Coriander. Matt's glasses blurred with tears. He put a finger into the matchbox. The ant crawled over his knuckle. 'Go on, sting me,' whispered Matt. 'What do I c-care?'

***

Coriander finished writing. She sighed and popped the letter into her pocket, ready for Charlie. He was so brave, smuggling out all her letters and posting them.

Coriander frowned. If he *was* posting them. How come she hadn't had any replies? Was Matt still angry with her after their argument? Surely not. And even if he was, why hadn't Perdita written back?

Coriander stroked Vinnie's dozy head. It *had* been a dreadful bust-up. Maybe Matt had told Perdita everything. Maybe Perdita was furious with her too. Maybe neither of them wanted to see her again.

No! Coriander grasped her left plait. There was always hope.

7

Hairies

Imagine a prune with a face. Imagine the wrinkled eyelids, sewn shut. Imagine puffy purple lips tied together by dangly bits of string. Imagine blue-black hair gushing from the crown like a too-big wig. Imagine a little triangular goatee beard dangling from the chin. And imagine the whole thing fitting into your hand.

Abbie didn't have to. She was looking at it.

'That. Is. Disgusting,' she gasped.

Perdita grinned. 'Well *you* wouldn't look so cute if you'd had your head cut off. And your skull taken out. And your scalp boiled. And hot stones shoved inside. Oh yes, *and* hot sand stuffed up your nostrils.'

'S'pose not,' mumbled Abbie.

'This was Mum's last find.' Perdita scoured her chin with her teeth. 'She picked it up in the Amazon jungle a few months ago. Actually she found two. But the other head fell out of a hole in her bag.'

Abbie felt a little sick. 'What do we have to do to it?'

'Darn it.'

'What's wrong?'

'No, I mean we have to darn it. Sew it up again. The stitches are all rotten.'

Abbie felt a bit sick.

'Come on. You hold the lips together while I unthread them. We wouldn't want the tongue to fall out, now would we?' Perdita chuckled.

Abbie didn't join in. The world went fuzzy as she reached out a finger and thumb and pinched the lips together gently. They felt surprisingly hard and smooth, like eggshell.

Perdita hummed as she pulled out the stitches. 'You can let go now.'

Abbie wished she hadn't. The lips lolled apart. Black flakes crumbled out of the mouth.

There was a low groan. 'Pardon me,' said Abbie. She backed away from the stand, holding her stomach.

Something whizzed past her feet. It was that grey furry something she'd seen the last time she came. She screamed.

'What?' asked Perdita, turning round.

'A rat!' gasped Abbie.

Perdita laughed. 'That's not a rat. That's Chester.' She reached out her hand and made sucky noises, as if calling in a cat for food. 'Chester,' she called, 'here Chess. Come and meet Abbie. She won't hurt you.'

The furry thing poked out from behind a stand. It crawled across the floor. Abbie got a proper look. What she'd thought was fur was actually a tangle of grey hair. It was changing shape all the time. One minute it was a thin rectangle, the next a triangle, the next a ball. It stopped at Abbie's feet and curled into a question mark. Then it jumped up and landed on her sleeve.

'Yeurrch!' Abbie shook her arm wildly. 'Get *OFF*!' The hairy thing leapt up, flew through the air and slammed into the wall behind the Hairyquarium. It clung there, shivering.

'Oh dear,' said Perdita. 'You've frightened him off. He's very sensitive. It's OK Chester.' She held out her hand again. The thing slid down the wall and crept across the floor to Perdita. It crawled up her leg and jumped into her palm. There it snuggled into a C-shape. Perdita stroked it gently. 'Feel him,' she said to Abbie. 'He can't bite – he hasn't got a mouth.'

Abbie stretched out a finger nervously. She touched the curls. They were soft and silky. 'What *is* it?'

'*He*,' corrected Perdita. 'Our pet. Dad found him. In hospital.'

'I see,' said Abbie faintly, not seeing at all.

'Two years ago Dad burned his hand. Tickling a toaster.'

'Like you do,' said Abbie, who'd never done anything of the sort.

'And he was waiting to see a nurse. There was this pile of grey hair on the floor. And it – *he* – jumped onto Dad's arm.'

'Of course,' said Abbie, as if it was the obvious place to jump.

'And when the nurse came in, he dived up Dad's sleeve.'

'Right,' said Abbie, as if she'd have done exactly the same thing.

'Left, actually. And Dad brought him home. Mum said he was a patch of chest hair. Probably shaved off an old man before an operation. So we named him Chester. He's the biggest help ever.' Perdita tickled him. 'Sweeping, dusting, cuddling us when we miss Mum. And he understands everything. Don't you Chess?' He squashed into a ball and bounced up and down on her palm. 'Now, come and say hello to Abbie.'

Chester the chest hair leapt onto Abbie's arm. He wriggled into her palm and made a heart shape. She laughed nervously. Then she stroked him.

Perdita turned back to the shrunken head. 'We'd better get on. I have to go and start cooking soon.' She pulled out a stitch from the left eyelid.

'Why do *you* have to cook?' Abbie had never baked so much as a bean for the Rotten Lot.

Perdita looked surprised. 'It's my job. No one else can do it. Auntie Mell's allergic to uncooked food. Uncle Dirk's got low blood sugar. He feels faint before meals. And Dad's always busy with whatever it is he's busy with. Now could you unthread the right eye?'

Abbie took a deep breath. She picked gingerly at a stitch. Chester made an encouraging sweatband round her wrist. 'So what exactly do they do all day, your aunt and uncle?' she asked.

'Auntie Mell prepares my lessons. She left school early

to become a beautician, so teaching's hard work for her. And Uncle Dirk's an accountant. He does the books for the museum.' From the state of the place, Abbie couldn't imagine that would take long. But Perdita explained he was setting things up for when the museum opened. 'Till then we have to live off Dad's Very Odd Job money. Mum used to do some hairdressing to pay for her trips, but of course that's dried up now.'

The girls unpicked the last stitches from the eyelids. There was another low groan.

'What?' asked Perdita.

'Wasn't me,' said Abbie, 'not this time, I swear.'

'To eswear ees no nice.'

The girls jumped back. Chester shot up Abbie's sleeve.

The head swivelled on its stand. The eyelids popped up. Black eyes glared at them.

'Who eswear?' said the hoarse voice. It was definitely coming from those lips.

Abbie and, for once, even Perdita were speechless.

'Qué?' said the head. 'You lose your tongues? Ees no excuse. I lose mine four hundred and thirty year ago. But now I espeak again. And I see again too.'

Perdita recovered first. 'Hello, um … Sir. My name's Perdita, and this is –'

The head wobbled irritably. 'Your names I know. Hokay I been blind. Hokay I been dumb. But my ears they leesten more than four centuries. To sigh of sloth in jungle. To poop of pirhana in river. To whoop of your mama when she find me. To talk in thees room since I arrive.'

'Who are – I mean who *were* you?' whispered Abbie. 'Before … ?' She didn't like to finish.

Chester poked out of her sleeve, trembling.

The head cleared its very short throat. 'I am Fernando Feraldo, Esplorer of Ecuador, Conquistador of Quito, Raider of Rainforest.' Then, in a smaller voice, 'And trophy of tribesmen.'

'What happened to you? Why did they – you know?' asked Perdita.

'The Jivaro tribe of Amazon, they shreenk my head. Because it too beeg. Because I theenk hokay to take their land in jungle for eSpain. Because I theenk hokay to steal their gold and make them eslaves.' A tear wandered down his lumpy cheek. 'I raid their land – and they raid my head. For my greed, you see, I shreenk to nobody. For my greed, you see, I *have* no body.'

'How terrible,' murmured Perdita. 'You poor thing.'

'No!' snapped Fernando. 'Thees I deserve. But my wife, she no deserve.'

'Your wife?' Abbie couldn't imagine this jumbo raisin being married. But what was new? She couldn't have imagined any of the things she'd seen over the last few days.

'My wife,' said Fernando, 'she tell me I wrong to raid Jivaro. She come weeth me. Try to estop me. And they shreenk her too.'

'The other head!' exclaimed Perdita. 'The one that fell out of Mum's bag!'

'Si.' The head nodded on its stand. 'Your mama, she find us both. And then she lose my ladylove. For four hundred and thirty year we have lie together on jungle floor. And then paff, my Senora, she gone – vamos!' More tears dribbled down his cheek. Chester – very bravely for a timid patch of chest hair – jumped onto Fernando's cheek to mop up the tears.

Abbie wasn't quite sure how to put the next question. Her curiosity had an inner chat with her delicacy. Delicacy got a kick in the pants. 'How come your, er, brain has, ah, lasted all these years?'

Fernando glared at her. 'How *I* suppose to know?'

Perdita's delicacy didn't even have pants. 'Probably all those hot stones,' she said cheerfully, 'rolling inside your head and preserving things.'

Fernando sniffed snootily. 'You lucky it preserve,' he said, 'for now it help you. Sewn into silence I theenk, I leesten. And now at last I espeak – so *you* must leesten.'

If he had a finger he'd wag it, thought Abbie.

'Do not talk of your mama before that woman. Or her man.'

Perdita frowned. 'You mean Auntie Mell and Uncle Dirk? Why ever not?'

'They up to no good.'

'What d'you mean?' asked Abbie.

Fernando flared his nostrils. 'You see these nosey holes? After all these year they smell all theengs. And aunt and uncle – hwaff.' He wrinkled his nose. 'They make beeg steenk. Of greed, of grab, of grasp.' He paused dramatically. 'Of conquering conquistador.'

Chester jumped onto Fernando's head and bounced up and down.

'The Curly One, he agree,' said Fernando.

'How dare you!' Perdita burst out. 'Auntie Mell's wonderful! And she's been fantastic since Mum left. Comforting me, cheering me up, when she's just as upset as I am. And Uncle Dirk's working so hard to get the museum on its feet.'

Fernando snorted. 'Pah! You and your father, *you* do all work here. And few days ago I hear them. Straight from – how you say? – horsie mouth.'

'What did you hear?' asked Abbie excitedly. Having grasped that a shrunken head could talk, she was keen to hear what it had to say.

'That morning,' said Fernando softly, his eyes darting round as if to check no one was eavesdropping, 'they in here, alone. Thees I know because I hear the uncle say, "Matt and Perdeeta, they gone for Very Odd Job".'

'Maybe that was the day you came to our house,' said Abbie.

'Then the aunt, she say, "Read this." Then I hear rustling. Then silence. Like someone reading. Then Dirk, he laugh. Sneaky snorty laugh, like thees – "Heh heh heh." And he say ...' Fernando paused like a bad actor ... 'he say, "*Good!*"'

It was Perdita's turn to snort. '"Good?" So blooming what?!'

Fernando shrugged. Or rather, he would have done if he'd had shoulders. 'Suit self,' he said, 'you do not have to believe. But I will watch them. When they look at me, I dead like thees.' He closed his eyes. 'And when they look away, I alive like thees.' His eyes sprang open. 'But you must not tell about me. If anyone find out, perhaps they sell me for freaky peep show. If I estay here, I can espy.'

'Thank you,' said Abbie.

Perdita wheeled round. 'You don't actually believe him, do you? You've never even met my uncle!'

Abbie hesitated. It wasn't exactly that she believed Fernando. More that she didn't know *what* to believe any more.

Perdita glowered at her. 'You'd better go. I have to make dinner.'

Anger flamed up Abbie's throat. 'Don't blame me!' she snapped. 'You show me all these crazy things, like hairy fish and Bobus hairs, and expect me to believe them. Then here comes another crazy thing and you expect me *not* to believe it! It's all so confusing.'

'You theenk I crazy theeng?' said Fernando huffily. 'I show you who crazy round here.' His face folded its arms.

'Look,' said Abbie, 'there's nothing to lose. If Fernando's wrong, your aunt and uncle have nothing to hide. And if he's right, then they might be hiding something about your mum. They might know if she's –'

'Of course she's still alive!' shouted Perdita. 'I keep telling you that. I don't need a nosey parker shrunken head to find out.'

'Well maybe you don't need me either!' yelled Abbie. 'Maybe you should go and look for your mum by yourself.' She grabbed the cell phone from her pocket and added meanly, 'I'm jolly well phoning mine. And I'll see myself out, thank you!'

She stormed towards the door, nearly knocking the Hairy Hoot off its stand. Chester scuttled after her and tugged her shoe. But she kicked him off. Before slamming the door she looked back to see Perdita clap her hands over her ears as Fernando declared, 'Thees nosey holes, they no lie.'

***

Matt heard a key turn in the lock. Footsteps cracked across the Hair Science floor. Then a hand clapped him on the shoulder and a voice said, 'How's it going, old fruit?'

Matt turned round. 'Hello Dirk. Still no luck, I'm afraid. I keep changing the potions and testing them. But how c-can I tell if they've worked, when all I c-can test them on is insects?'

'Good point.' Dirk rubbed his chin. 'What you need is a

bigger animal to be your guinea pig. Like for instance … a guinea pig!' He clapped Matt on the shoulder again.

Matt shook his head fiercely. 'No! I c-couldn't possibly do tests on anything c-cuddly. It wouldn't feel right.'

'Hmm.' Dirk frowned. 'Leave it with me, old bean. I'll think of a way round this.'

***

'Eat your carrots, Minnie,' said Coriander. 'Remember they'll help you see in the dark.' Minnie stuck a carrot in her ear.

'I said *see*, not *hear*, you little monkey!'

Across the room Winnie frowned indignantly. Monkey indeed!

8

Fishy business

'Nothing,' muttered Abbie, as Mum asked for the third time what she'd done to upset Perdita. 'We had an argument. It's not always *my* fault, you know.'

'She's so nice. If I can help you sort it out …' Mum glanced into the rear view mirror. The look Abbie gave her could have gone into the washing machine and still come out dirty.

By the time they got home, though, it *was* sorted out: in Abbie's mind, at least. Perdita shouldn't have shouted. But things were so hard for her. And Fernando's claim that her aunt and uncle were up to something must be shocking. Aunt Melliflua – with all her 'plumcakes' and arms round shoulders – *was* looking after Perdita (even if it was in a 'cook my dinner, sweetie' sort of way). And Uncle Dirk *was* helping to run the museum (even if it was in a losing money sort of way).

Anyway, never mind *them*, Abbie had to make it up with

Perdita. No way was she going to lose this whacky new friend. Or her trip to Spain. There was only one thing to do.

But saying sorry wasn't easy. Abbie needed some help. Some encouragement. Some biscuits.

She sneaked into the kitchen, grabbed some ginger nuts from the tin, crept past Ollie in the sitting-room and dashed upstairs, her shirt bulging.

'Muuum,' Ollie's voice curled upstairs like a bad smell, 'Abbie took four biscuits.'

Abbie shoved them under her duvet and ran onto the landing. 'Did not!' she yelled.

But Mum was already in her bedroom. 'Oh really?' she said, pulling back the duvet.

'I took five.'

Mum's left hand clasped Bob. She looked at Abbie for a long time. Then, without a word, she gathered the biscuits and went downstairs.

Abbie waited until she was in the kitchen then tore down to the sitting-room. Ollie was on the sofa colouring in a picture.

Abbie jostled his elbow so that the felt pen went over the line. 'Creepie crawlie,' she whispered. Just as he opened his mouth to howl the phone rang.

'I'll get it!' they both shouted. They wrestled on the sofa until Ollie slipped out from under Abbie.

'Fine,' he said down the phone. 'How are *you*?'

Who was it? Ollie never had polite chats on the phone.

'I drawed a card for you,' he said. 'But Abbie messed

it up.' Abbie looked at his picture. A tall wonky girl was playing ball with a small wonky boy. The girl's mouth was wider than her face. The boy had curly hair.

'Yes.' Ollie giggled. 'But you won't catch me. I'll wear my magic boots.'

Heat whooshed up Abbie's throat, as if she'd swallowed a hot drink upside down. How dare her brother have fun with her friend? How dare her friend have fun with her brother?

'Abbie,' called Ollie. 'It's Perdita.'

'I know that, you flea.' Abbie grabbed the phone.

'Abbie?' came Perdita's voice. 'I'm really sorry. I shouldn't have flown at you. I was just so mad when Fernando accused my aunt and uncle.'

Abbie's throat cooled. 'It's OK. I'm sorry too. And look, there's no proof, just Fer–' she broke off. Ollie was suddenly having great trouble opening the sitting-room door. 'Let's just wait and see.'

'OK. So you're still on?'

'Course I am.'

'Thanks. Hey, Dad's paid me for mending the shrunken head. I've got your money too. And guess what, he said it looks great, you can't even see the stitches.' She giggled. 'Wonder why. I'd better go. I've got to help Dad with the washing up.'

'Do you have to do that too?'

'Auntie Mell's allergic to detergent. And Uncle Dirk has to lie down after dinner or he gets dizzy. Can you come round tomorrow? I'm sure there'll be another job for us.'

'Sure.' Abbie guessed that Mum would be glad for her to go. She ended the call then went into the kitchen to ask.

Mum was washing lettuce. 'Course you can, darling. I'm so pleased you've made it up with Perdita. Now, would you lay the table, please?'

Abbie was just about to make a face when she thought of Perdita cooking, clearing and washing up. Her face stayed unmade and the table was laid.

Next morning, as Abbie was putting her shoes on, Ollie came into the hall. 'Can I come too?' he asked. 'I want to give my card to Perdita.'

Abbie rolled her eyes. 'You're not invited.'

Dad came downstairs. 'I'm sure Abbie'll pass your card on,' he said. 'I'll take you, Abbs. Matt said he'd give me a quick tour of the museum.'

Abbie stared at him.

'I just phoned Matt to ask if I could bring round Mum's bedside lamp,' he said. 'The switch doesn't work.'

'But …' Abbie's stomach met her feet.

'A quick tour,' Dad repeated firmly.

Matt and Perdita were waiting by the gate. They led the way across the field to the museum.

As they passed the balding bush, Dad gave it a pat. 'Know how you feel, mate,' he chuckled.

'You're embarrassing me,' hissed Abbie.

Matt went first through the archway, then Perdita, then

Dad. Halfway up the first flight of stairs he turned round and grinned. 'Isn't this great, Abbs?' She couldn't help grinning back. He was like a great galumphing puppy with his tongue hanging out.

On the first landing Matt gazed at the wonky 'Hairstory' sign. 'Must fix that,' he murmured.

Of all the things that need fixing, thought Abbie. But what she said was, 'You're going to love this, Dad.'

And of course he did. The girls watched him stone-the-crows his way round the room.

'Let's leave them to it,' whispered Perdita.

Abbie followed her upstairs. 'What if your dad tells mine everything?' she said.

'What's there to tell? Dad doesn't know our plan. The worst he can say is that Mum's gone missing. And your dad'll be so busy asking questions they probably won't even get round to that. Come on. We're going to clean the Hairyquarium.'

They rested on the second landing. Abbie leaned against the door to Hair Science. A grey mat slid out under the door and shot up her leg. 'Hi Chester,' she said. He settled on her shoulder and nuzzled her cheek. She breathed in his talcum powder scent.

On the third landing Perdita pulled out a bag from her pocket. 'Want some?'

Without thinking Abbie took a handful. The dry bubbles crackled on her tongue, crisp as bacon and crunchy as toast. 'What are they?'

'Lice crispies. Full of protein.'

Abbie spat them onto the floor. Funny how good they'd tasted till now.

Perdita opened the door to Rare Hair. Abbie was about to go over and greet Fernando when she saw two figures on the far side of the room. Their backs were turned. They were looking at the Hairyquarium. Chester dived down the front of Abbie's T-shirt. The figures turned round.

'Halloo sweetie pies.' Aunt Melliflua waved.

'Bouncing bullion!' growled the man next to her. 'You gave us a fright.'

'Sorry Uncle Dirk,' said Perdita. 'This is my friend Abbie.'

Uncle Dirk grunted: a hard grey grunt to go with his hard grey hairstyle.

The girls joined them at the fish tank.

'So calming, aren't they?' sighed Aunt Melliflua. 'We were just admiring them.'

'We've come to clean them out,' said Perdita.

'Good show, girls,' said Uncle Dirk. He raised the glass he was holding and sipped a colourless liquid. Abbie got the feeling it probably wasn't water.

From head to trouser hems, Uncle Dirk was grey. His eyes were slaty and bored. His thin face was ashen. His suit gleamed like wet concrete. But his shoes! They twinkled up at Abbie, poppy red and pointy. And, from the way he parted them slightly as she looked, Abbie could tell that Uncle Dirk was very proud of his footwear.

'We'll leave you to it, angel cakes,' said Melliflua. 'You

know I'm allergic to cleaning fluids. Come Dirkie.' She took his elbow and steered him out of the room.

When they'd gone Chester poked out of the top of Abbie's T-shirt.

'Why did you hide, Chess?' asked Abbie.

Perdita stroked his grey curls. 'Auntie Mell and Uncle Dirk didn't really take to Chester when they came to live here. They thought he was a bit –' she cupped her hands round her mouth so he wouldn't see and whispered – '*icky.*' She took her hands away. 'And they asked if we'd –' she cupped again – '*get rid of him.* So we pretended to. They don't know he's still here.'

No wonder he's not their biggest fan, thought Abbie. She went across to their other not-biggest fan. Fernando's face was dead as a doll's. She tugged his hair gently. 'It's OK. They've gone.'

His eyelids sprang up. He glared round the room. 'Hoot!' he snapped.

'Good morning to you too,' said Perdita huffily. 'Yes thank you, I slept very well.'

'The senorita, she steell angry,' said Fernando to Abbie. 'But now she see. Look in Hootie beak.'

Frowning, Abbie went over to the Hairy Hoot. She lifted the flap at the front of the beak. The tube was hollow. She ran her fingers round the inside wall to check – and felt the last thing she expected. She pulled it out.

'Hah!' crowed Fernando. 'You see? Just now, Melliflua she show thees to Dirk. And she say, "Here. Another one arrive today." And Dirk he read it. Then he say, "How these are getting out?" And Melliflua she say, "I no idea. But never mind *how* – they good news. They tell us she steell there. They help us keep an eye on her." Fernando paused dramatically. 'Then you senoritas come to door. So Dirk he shove thees in Hootie beak for hide. And they pretend look at feesh.'

'Give it here!' Perdita ran over and snatched the toilet roll from Abbie. She began to unravel the pink tissue. 'Oh!' she gasped. 'It's Mum's writing! Dated 28 July – that's yesterday!'

'*My darling Matt and Perdita,*' she read. She stopped. Her top teeth scoured her chin. A tear bulged from her eye and dropped onto the toilet paper.

Abbie put her hand on Perdita's shoulder. Chester jumped over to dab her eyes.

Perdita continued. '*I hope you're both well. I think of you all the time and wonder why you haven't written. It's now ten weeks and six days since I was –*'

'Hide!' snapped Fernando. Chester plunged down the back of Perdita's neck as the door to Rare Hair opened. Abbie snatched the loo roll from Perdita and shoved it into her pocket. Fernando shut his face down.

'Almost forgot.' Aunt Melliflua's head wafted round the door. 'Lunch at one, please, Perdie.' She leaned forward to look at Perdita. 'You all right, apple pie?'

'Fine,' Perdita mumbled.

Abbie thought fast. They had to finish reading that letter. Now.

'Actually,' she said, 'my mum's invited Perdita for lunch. She's already bought all the stuff.' For good measure she added, 'My grandma's all excited. And cancellations make her ill.' It wasn't exactly a lie. Squashy threw a right wobbly whenever Bingo was called off.

Perdita sniffed. 'Th-that's right, Auntie. There's bread in the cupboard for sandwiches.'

'But –' Melliflua frowned – 'what about *making* them, sweetie? You know I get a rash spreading butter.'

'Try margarine,' said Abbie helpfully. She ushered Perdita past her aunt and through the door. Then, fingering the loo roll in her pocket, Abbie thought again. 'Or maybe you could go out for lunch.' That would keep Melliflua and Dirk out of the way for longer.

'Might just do that,' murmured Melliflua, as the girls headed downstairs.

***

Matt finished trimming Samson's beard.

'How often do you do that?' said Dad.

'Oh every day. Twice sometimes.'

'I just can't … I mean … I'm speechless,' said Dad, who'd talked non-stop for the last half hour. 'This place is just –'

'Look, I'm sorry, but I'd better get back to work. It'll be lunch soon. I c-can show you the rest of the museum another time if you're interested.'

'*Interested?* I've never been so interested in all my life! This beats the Pyramids at dawn! The Parthenon by moonlight! This is … Living History! This is … The Past in Pigtails! This is … Abbie!'

'Hi Dad.' She poked her head round the door. 'Can Perdita come for lunch, Mr Platt?'

***

Coriander scraped out the last bit of melon flesh with her teeth. 'Delicious.' She wiped her mouth and handed the peel to Vinnie. He chewed it loudly.

'Anyone for grapes?' Coriander held up the bunch. Winnie nodded from across the room.

'Ready?' said Coriander. Winnie opened her mouth. It was nearly as big as Perdita's.

'Catch.' Coriander threw a grape. Winnie caught it between her very large teeth.

9

Smudges

Dad smacked the steering wheel. 'Genius!' he bellowed. 'Your dad's a genius!'

'Keep it down, Dad,' said Abbie from the back seat. 'Perdita's right behind you.'

'You never told me it was *real* hair, Abbs!' Dad went on. 'Can you believe it? I touched Einstein's eyebrows!' He whooped with delight. The car veered onto the pavement.

'Watch out, Dad!'

A mother lifted her hand from a pushchair to make a rude sign.

Dad waved an apology and swerved back onto the road. 'I stroked Henry the Eighth's beard!' Beating a rhythm on the steering wheel, he sang:

I stroked his beard –
His weirdy beard
So red and fat –
How cool is that?

'Dad?'

'Yes love?'

'Shut up.'

But Perdita was smiling for the first time since they'd found the letter. 'You like our museum then, Mr Hartley?'

'Like it?' He swivelled round in the driving seat. 'Like it?'

'Dad!' yelled Abbie as the wing mirror pinged against a lamp-post.

'Sorry.' He turned back to the front. 'It's fantabulent. It's magnificous. It's …'

'… Probably better not to tell Mum,' said Abbie.

Dad sighed. 'I know what you mean. She might not quite – what's the word? – *appreciate* it.' He paused. 'She would've done once, you know.'

Abbie snorted. 'Not since I was born.'

'Maybe. But when I met her she loved a bit of oddity.'

'You're joking.'

'Your mother,' declared Dad, 'once took me ice skating in pyjamas. She once hung our cutlery on the washing line. She once,' he smacked his knee, 'dug a hole in the garden and planted herself.'

'Why?' asked Abbie.

'To see how it felt to be a tree. But when you were born she got all sort of –'

'Boring?'

Dad laughed. 'That's a bit harsh. I was going to say worried. Worried about being a good mother. About keeping up appearances, doing normal mum things. Dieting, ironing your socks, making yoghurt.'

'That's not normal,' said Abbie, picturing the sludge in her lunch box. 'That's sick.'

At the front door Perdita was clamped in an Ollie hug. Her eyes darted between Abbie's face and pocket, while Ollie explained that he and Mum were making her a 'special lunch'.

As soon as Perdita had unhooked herself from Ollie, the girls ran into the garden and made for the treehouse. Abbie scrambled up after Perdita. She stood on the platform and fished out the toilet roll from her pocket. Chester wriggled out from under Perdita's T-shirt, where he'd been hiding since the last conversation with Melliflua. He jumped onto her shoulder, ready for hanky duty.

They sat down carefully on the wonky planks. 'You'd better not stay too long,' said Abbie. 'You need to put the letter back in the Hoot's beak. Your aunt and uncle might look for it when they get back from lunch.'

Perdita nodded and, with shaking hands, peeled back the loo roll. It wasn't easy. The tissue had gone lumpy from her tears. She took a deep breath and carried on from where she'd left off. '*It's now ten weeks and six days since I was …* No!' Perdita clapped a hand to her mouth.

'What?' whispered Abbie, peering over her shoulder.

'*Kidnapped!*' Perdita let out a sob. She read on. '*And still you haven't answered my letters. I'm so frightened you're not at the museum any more, that you've been kidnapped too. But*

I hope and plait every day, trusting that you're OK. That I was the only one taken that night. The only one to feel those gloved hands across my mouth and that blanket over my head. The only one to be pushed into that waiting car.' Perdita looked up. Tears streaked her cheeks. Abbie squeezed her arm.

'*So here I am at … Oh no,'* wailed Perdita. 'I've smudged it!' Her tears flowed faster. Chester leapt into action, dabbing her eyes. But it was too late.

'Something something … oh it's all blurred … *keep me company. But they just remind me of …* something … *and how much I mi …* something something. *Please please write. But remember, you must addr …* oh no! Look what I've done!' Perdita put her head in her hands.

Abbie took the loo roll. The next section was a splodge of tears and ink. Chester lay over the sheet, trying to dry the smudges. But the damage was done.

Abbie squinted at the tissue. '*Remember, you must addr* … something … *Ch* … something … *at B* something.' Underneath she read, '*All my* … something, *Cor* … something.' At the bottom were lots of fuzzy kisses.

Perdita looked up. 'I've ruined it. The address.' Her face crumpled again.

Abbie moved the loo roll out of the way of Perdita's tears. She read over what she could. 'We need to copy this out. Wait.'

She jumped down from the tree. Two minutes later she was back with a sheet of paper and a pen. She copied out the letter, putting question marks where she couldn't make out the words. Perdita watched through her tears, scraping her chin with her teeth and tugging her plaits. Chester hovered between her eyes and nose. Every now and then he jumped onto a branch to shake himself free of tears, like a dog after a swim.

Abbie held up the copied-out letter. 'I've guessed some of the words and underlined them,' she said.

Perdita sniffed.

So here I am at ????????????? keep me company. But they just remind me of <u>family</u> and how much I <u>miss you</u>. Please please write. But remember, you must <u>address it to</u> Ch???? at B??????.

All my love forever,
Coriander xxxxxxxxxxxx

'But we still haven't got the address,' moaned Perdita.

Abbie frowned. 'Well, we know it's "Ch something" at "B something". Maybe "Ch something" is a name. If she's been kidnapped, perhaps she's saying the letter has to be addressed to someone else. Someone who's helping her. Maybe the same person who smuggled this letter out.'

'And "B something"?'

'That must be the place.' Abbie peered at the loo roll again. 'I think it's two words. B something, then a shorter word.'

'Is that "g" and "h"?' asked Perdita, squinting at the end of the first word.

Abbie chewed her pen. Then she shouted, 'Bradleigh!'

Perdita jostled forward to get a better look. 'No … d'you think so?' She sprang up, nearly knocking Abbie out of the tree. 'So all this time Mum's been in a town twenty miles away. When I thought she was cavorting with castanets. That's incredible!' She threw her arms wide. A grin ripped her face. 'Brilliant! Fantastic!' She danced on the planks. They groaned alarmingly. 'Mum, Mum, here we come!'

'Hang on a sec,' said Abbie, spreading her palms either side to steady the planks. 'There must be loads of places beginning with Bradleigh. Bradleigh Library, Bradleigh Sports Centre, Bradleigh Cinema … we've got to work out the second word.'

Perdita went still. Air seemed to leak out of her. She flopped down next to Abbie. 'We'll never find Mum.' Her head drooped.

'Don't give up now!' cried Abbie.

Perdita's shoulders drooped.

'What about these?' Abbie pointed to her plaits.

The plaits drooped.

'Oh come on!' Abbie hit a plank.

The plank drooped. For goodness sake, when would Mr Platt come and fix this treehouse?

Mr Platt. The Very Odd Job Man.

The Very Odd Job Man from the phone book.

'The phone book,' murmured Abbie. It was worth a try.

They didn't have a chance to look before lunch. But Abbie was glad to see that Perdita had perked up. She was helping Squashy look for her glasses in the hall. Abbie laid the table and watched them through the kitchen door.

'Where did you last see them?' Perdita was asking.

'How could I *see* 'em if I wasn't wearing 'em to *see*?' barked Squashy.

Chester, who'd disguised himself as a belt round Perdita's waist, suddenly jumped onto Grandma's head. He pushed her wig off. Her glasses were underneath, perched on the mouldy wisps of her real hair.

'Whassat?' Squashy's hand flew to her head.

'Chester,' said Perdita.

Grandma grabbed him by the curls. Watching through the kitchen door, Abbie held her breath. What on earth would the grumpy old grumbleguts make of Chester?

Grandma dangled him in front of her face. She pushed her glasses onto her nose and peered at him for a long time. Then she said, 'Pleased to meet you, Chester. Cuddly little chap, aren't you?' Abbie grinned. You had to hand it to Squashy: it would take more than wriggling chest hair to rattle her trolley.

'Don't let Mum see him,' Abbie whispered. 'She'll have a fit. Hey Grandma, he likes you.' Chester gave a little bounce then dived back down to belt business.

Lunch was quiche and ham and crusty white bread and cold sausage and lemonade and all those things Mum only did for visitors. Abbie was glad. It was about time someone made a fuss of Perdita.

Not that Perdita really noticed. When she wasn't pouring salt on her bread or ketchup on her thumb, she was scraping her teeth over her chin and drumming her fingers on the table.

Abbie got the message. 'We'll clear up and make some coffee,' she said as soon as everyone had finished. 'You go into the sitting-room. We'll bring it in.'

'How kind,' said Mum. 'I can see you're having a good influence, Perdita.' Abbie's mind stuck its tongue out at Mum.

'I'll help,' said Ollie.

'No,' said Perdita hurriedly. 'You go with your mum and dad and I'll bring you a special treat.' Ollie giggled. *There they go again*, thought Abbie. *Good as married.*

The grown ups and Ollie went into the sitting-room. Abbie closed the door and fetched the phone book from the hall table.

Perdita was already peering at the loo roll in the kitchen. Abbie plonked the phone book on the table and began to thumb through the business section. When she got to the 'Br' page Chester jumped off Perdita's waist and stretched up the centre of the double page like a bookmark.

'So, the first word's "Bradleigh".' Abbie studied the toilet roll. 'And the second word looks short.' Her eyes skimmed down the page. 'Bradleigh Blinds?' She studied the toilet roll. 'Naah. The second word begins with a spiky letter. Bradleigh Inn? Nope, it's wider than an I. Looks more like a …' She muttered her way down the list until … she jabbed the page triumphantly.

Perdita shoved her face over Abbie's shoulder. '*Zoo?!*'

'Look.' Abbie pointed at the loo roll. 'The first letter of the second word could easily be Z. And the only Z with "Bradleigh" in front of it is "Zoo"!' Chester bounced round the table.

Perdita looked from the phone book to the toilet roll and back. 'Well …' she bit her inside cheek. 'I see what you mean. Yes!'

'There's the number. Go on. You can use the phone in Mum and Dad's room. Everyone'll hear you in the hall.'

'Will you do it?' asked Perdita. 'I'm shaking too much.'

Chester slipped under Perdita's T-shirt. The girls crept upstairs with the phone book and tiptoed across the landing.

Abbie closed the door softly and sat on Mum and Dad's bed. Perdita sat on top of her.

'Shove over,' hissed Abbie.

'Sorry. Not thinking,' mumbled Perdita, moving away. Abbie held the receiver between them and dialled the number. Her heart thundered in her ears. She could hardly hear the ring tone.

After ten rings a woman's voice answered, 'Bradleigh Zoo. Can I help you?'

'Hello,' croaked Abbie. Her throat felt full of sand. 'May I speak to Coriander Platt please?'

There was a pause. Just a little one.

'Who?'

'Mrs Coriander Platt?'

Another pause.

'No one of that name here.'

'Are you sure? I think she might be working there.'

'No. I'd remember a name like that. Who am I speaking to?'

Abbie slammed the phone down. Her hands were trembling so much it took her ages to replace the receiver.

Perdita grabbed her arm. 'D'you think she's there?'

'I don't know. And if she *is*, phoning was a bad idea. They're not exactly going to be parading her with the penguins if she was kidnapped, are they? She's bound to be hidden away. I'll have to go there and snoop around.'

Perdita squeezed her wrist. 'I'll come too.'

'No, we've been through this. You can't go. You've got to

stay at home and pretend everything's normal.'

'But I can't,' moaned Perdita.

'Got to,' said Abbie. 'Look, you told me your dad couldn't handle it if you went missing. Plus, if your aunt and uncle are involved – which I'm not saying they *are* – you can't just disappear. You have to go back and act normal. Otherwise they might –' Abbie shrugged – 'well, I dunno. But you've got to pretend nothing's changed.'

Perdita grabbed a bedspread frill. 'They *can't* be involved, they just *can't*. Why would they be? I mean –' she rubbed the lace miserably between her fingers – 'Auntie Mell is mum's *sister*!'

And Henry the Eighth was Anne Boleyn's husband, thought Abbie, *but that didn't stop him reorganising her head*. What she said, though, was, 'Look, we don't know anything for sure. Let's not worry about it till I've been to Bradleigh Zoo.'

'Shouldn't we go to the police?'

'And say what? That we suspect your aunt and uncle? On the evidence of a soggy loo roll and a shrunken head? Oh, sure. They'd love it.'

'What about Dad then?' said Perdita.

'Go ahead. He'll either have a nervous breakdown or tell my dad. Or both. Let me just go to the zoo. If I don't find anything, there's nothing to tell. And if I do, you can tell who you like.'

'How can you go without your parents knowing?'

'Hmm.' Abbie frowned at the carpet. Then she looked up and grinned. 'Easy.'

She explained her plan. Perdita hugged her. 'You're brilliant.'

'Tell me that when I've found your mum,' said Abbie. 'Now come on. We'd better go and make that coffee. You've got to get back with the loo roll.'

They stole back down to the kitchen. Abbie washed the dishes and Chester dried. Perdita took a little bottle from her pocket and poured a few drops into a glass of water. 'Ollie's treat,' she explained.

Abbie raised her eyebrows in a you're-going-to-tell-me-anyway-so-I-won't-bother-asking sort of way.

'Fruits of the Forest hairspray. Delicious.'

***

The door to Hair Science opened. Dirk popped his head round. 'Just to let you know,' he called to Matt, 'I've been doing the accounts. Funds are at rock bottom, I'm afraid. Need to get a move on with those tests, old bean. See you later.'

He closed the door. Matt poured his latest potion over the earthworm that was wriggling across his desk. Tiny bumps sprang up all over the creature's body.

Matt threw up his hands in exasperation. 'How do I know if bumps are a sign of beauty in earthworms?' He picked the worm up and headed for the door. 'C-come on,' he murmured, 'I'll take you back outside.' He chewed his lip. 'To be with your family.'

***

Coriander watched Winnie and Minnie creep through the door. They stole up to Vinnie who was asleep in the corner. Minnie tickled his nostril with a piece of straw. Then Winnie planted a great sloppy kiss on his cheek. Vinnie snorted awake.

Coriander chewed her lip. 'How lovely,' she murmured, 'to be with your family.'

10

Sleepover

Mum and Dad were delighted to hear that Perdita had invited Abbie to stay the night.

'It'll do you good to get away from your brother,' said Mum. Abbie couldn't agree more. She'd been at war with Ollie ever since Perdita had left. It started when Matt came to the door to collect her.

Ollie had hugged Perdita goodbye and said, 'I wish *you* were my sister.'

Fury ripped through Abbie. 'I wish she was *mine* and *you* weren't born!' Mum sent her to her room. On the landing she tripped over the eggbox tortoise Ollie had made that morning.

'Stupid thing,' she said, kicking it.

When Ollie came upstairs and saw the crumpled eggbox he burst into tears and said he hated Abbie ... who opened her bedroom door to say what a coincidence, she felt the same about Ollie ... who spent the next ten minutes sitting on the landing so he could tell on Abbie if she sneaked out for biscuits.

Dad said it was like the Siege of Troy.

Mum said she was sick of them both, she was going to get her eyebrows waxed.

Squashy said kids of today, what they needed – but no one got to hear what they needed because, just then, a lady from the library phoned to say that Squashy had left her purse behind.

'My family, they're the pits,' said Abbie the next afternoon. She was climbing over the gate into the museum field.

Perdita was waiting on the other side. 'Why? I think they're great.' She waved Dad off. He turned in his seat to wave back, narrowly missing a tree.

Perdita hoicked Abbie's overnight bag over her shoulder and strode across the field. 'Bet your mum helped you pack this,' she said pointedly.

'Too right.' Abbie held up her hand and worked it like a nagging mouth. '"*Have you got your toothbrush ... don't forget spare knickers ... you can't wear those trousers ... take my cell phone.*" She nearly found the Custard Creams I wrapped in my pyjamas, too.'

Perdita didn't seem to have heard. 'Bet Ollie'll miss you tonight.'

'Give me a break! It's *you* he misses. If I was run over by a bus he'd tell Mum I'd crossed the road without looking.'

'Maybe he's just trying to get his own back. Coz he thinks you don't like him.'

'Maybe he's right. Coz Mum likes him enough for two.'

'Maybe she's just protecting him. Coz you're bigger.'

'Maybe you should mind your own –' Abbie bit her lip. The last thing she wanted was another fight. 'Hey, wait for me!'

Perdita's pants were swarming with ants today. By the time Abbie reached the museum door she'd already climbed three stairs. She looked round. 'Sorry. I'm just so nervous. What did you say?'

Abbie caught her up. 'I said, how did you manage to get your aunt and uncle out of the way?'

Perdita giggled. 'I told them Samson's got headlice. I knew that'd scare them off. They won't be back till I've treated all the hair in the museum. And you'll be gone by then. There's a bus at three. Let's go and find Chester.'

They climbed up past Hairstory and Hair Science. On the third landing Perdita opened the door to Rare Hair. Chester was inside, dusting the case of the Bobus hair. He jumped onto Abbie's head. Then he shot back to the Bobus case and rubbed till the glass squeaked.

'He's nearly done,' said Perdita. 'I told you he's a great worker.'

A faint snoring sound was coming from the back of the room. The girls went over to Fernando's stand.

Perdita tapped the top of his head. 'Wakey wakey.'

He opened one eye. 'Qué? Eh, pardone. I dream of rainforest. Of love and leaves.'

'Of what?' said Abbie.

He yawned. 'Of my love. My life. The wife who I leaved. Who I left in the leafs. No, leaved in the lefts – oh, thees Eengleesh!' If he'd had a hand he would have smacked his head. Instead he took a deep breath. 'My wife who I love. And I leafed in the leafs.'

'We understand,' said Abbie, patting his head. 'You miss your wife.'

'You *no* understand!' Fernando's beetle eyes glittered. 'My wife she my life. Four hundred and thirty year we roll together on forest floor. Oh,' his head wobbled so wretchedly it nearly fell off the stand, 'I am sad bad man.'

'No,' said Abbie gently. 'You're a sad *good* man. Look how you're helping us.'

Perdita crouched down till her eyes were level with his. She cupped him in her hands. 'I'm sorry for shouting at you, Fernando. You've given us our only lead to Mum.'

Fernando gave a moan that would have split his guts, if he'd had any. 'Oh my Carmen, my adored Senora. She gone for ever.'

At five to three the girls were standing at the bus stop on the main road.

Perdita hugged Abbie ferociously. 'You're the best.' She pressed three five pound notes and some coins into her hand. 'That should be plenty, for the zoo and snacks and –' she

gave a little hop, 'two single bus tickets back!' She squeezed Abbie's hand. 'Make sure you ask the driver where to get off. And make sure you don't miss the last bus back. And make sure –'

'My hand doesn't fall off. You're worse than Mum,' said Abbie, pulling her arm away.

Perdita gripped her wrist. 'You'll phone me as soon as you find anything, won't you?'

'Course. But what if your aunt or uncle answers? Or your dad? I wish you had a cell phone.'

'I'll try to get the phone whenever it rings. And if anyone else does, just pretend you're phoning from your house,' said Perdita.

The bus pulled up. Perdita shoved an old ice cream box into Abbie's hands. 'To keep you going.'

Abbie found a seat and put the box on her lap. She waved out of the window until Perdita was nothing more than a prancing spider in the distance.

Abbie leaned her head against the itchy seat. She'd managed to keep pretty calm in front of Perdita. First rule of journalism, stay cool. But now her stomach was filling with trampolining crickets.

A little nibble: that would settle her nerves. But the Custard Creams were in the bottom of her bag. Cautiously she opened the lid of the ice cream box. There was a bottle of Fruits of the Forest hairspray and a pile of sandwiches. Without thinking she took a bite of bread. It was smeared with pink foam. At the bottom of the box, on a paper serviette, Perdita had written *Magimousse. Stiffens hair and nerves.*

'Bleuhh,' Abbie spluttered.

The lady in front turned round in her seat. 'Poor love. My Waldo's the same on buses. Here.' She handed Abbie a paper bag.

'It's OK, I'm fine.' Abbie suddenly realised that the only thing making her sick was the *thought* of eating hair mousse. It *tasted* wonderful and had knocked out the crickets. She polished off three sandwiches, leaned back again and closed her eyes. Her hand cupped the right pocket of her jacket.

But not even Chester's reassuring wriggles could stop Abbie's worries from worming back. What if they'd got it wrong? What if the address was Bradleigh Zips, which wasn't in the phone book? That pause on the phone yesterday: had she imagined it? And if not, what on earth was she heading into?

***

There was a knock at the door of Hair Science.

'Dad?' came Perdita's voice from the other side. Matt grabbed the tangle of golden hair on his desk and shoved it into a drawer underneath. He ran to the door and opened it a slit.

'Hi Dad. I just wondered if you needed any jobs doing.'

Matt frowned. 'Are you all right, Perdie? You look a bit flushed.'

'I'm fine. Just been for a – a walk.'

104

'Well,' Matt rubbed his teeth, taking care not to open the door too widely. 'You c-could trim the bushes. I noticed a few split ends on the bunches.'

'Sure.' And before Matt could thank her she was gone.

***

Coriander made her bed for the fourth time. This was the worst part of the day: mid-afternoon. Vinnie, Winnie and Minnie were out the front having fun. And she was stuck in here, without so much as a crisp packet to read.

Coriander lay on the bed. She closed her eyes and tried to imagine she was in the kitchen baking dandruff biscuits with Perdita.

Her eyes sprang open. Was it one egg or two you needed? No – she was forgetting the recipe! Perdita, too, was fading in her mind to a blank face with plaits. Coriander clasped her head. She had to get out of here – and soon.

11

Schnik

'Next stop Bradleigh Zoo.' The bus driver looked over his shoulder at Abbie. She couldn't decide if his fringe was too long or his face too short.

She finished her sandwiches and half the Fruits of the Forest hairspray. Burping delicately, she packed the rest in her rucksack and got off the bus.

It was a scowly smiley afternoon. The air was warm and humid. Clouds like old men's eyebrows frowned across the sky. The minute Abbie unzipped her jacket the sun went in. The minute she zipped it up the sun came out.

Her mood, too, was all over the place. If the bus hadn't dropped her right outside the zoo, and if the queue hadn't been moving so fast, she might well have got back on. Did she really *want* to find Coriander? Sniffing out Bourbons in the kitchen was one thing, sniffing out lost mothers quite another.

But she was here now, with loads of ice cream money.

Might as well have a wander. It could even be quite fun, imagining which animal she'd choose for a pet. It was years since she'd been here. Mum had sworn never to return after Ollie had got lost for two and a quarter minutes outside the reptile house and Abbie had pointed out the llama poo to four old ladies.

She arrived at the entrance hut.

'£5 love,' yawned the woman behind the window. Even the cigarette dangling from her lips looked bored. She didn't notice – or care – that Abbie was on her own.

Abbie pushed the money through the gap under the window. She took a deep breath. ''Scuse me. Does a lady called Coriander Platt work here?'

The lady tapped the cigarette on an ashtray. 'Coriander? That's an 'erb, innit?' She squawked with laughter. 'Not that I know of, love. Mind you, I only been 'ere a week. I dunno anyone. The boss 'asn't even bovvered to show me rahnd. You'd fink 'e'd 'ave the manners … we close at six, dear.' She pressed a buzzer. The tall entrance gate opened.

'Thanks,' said Abbie. That gave her two hours to snoop round. She went through the gate. The lady hadn't noticed she'd gone and was still grumbling away.

There were toilets on the left, a shop on the right and a pond in front. Flamingos rose from the water like snooty question marks. Ducks wove between them.

Abbie looked round for someone official. But there was only an old couple eating apples on a bench and a mother with a boy in a pushchair. The mother was feeding the ducks.

The boy was shoving an ice cream at every bit of his face except his mouth. Abbie thought of Ollie. She could be at home now making him cry. She chewed her sleeve. Not that she missed him, of course, or anyone else for that matter. It was just that she'd never been anywhere without the Rotten Lot knowing about it, and the crickets were stirring in her stomach again. What she needed was a spot of blood sugar.

She went to the shop and bought a double choc chip ice cream with double flakes and double chocolate sauce. Then she came out and sat on the bench next to the old couple.

'Nice day,' said the man, fanning himself with his cap.

'Mmm,' said Abbie, licking ice cream off her jacket.

'Have you lost someone, dear?' said the lady, whose hair was like a cauliflower.

'Oh – no. My mum's feeding the elephants with my brother.' Abbie liked the sound of that.

The man eyed her ice cream. 'That looks good,' he murmured.

'Mmm,' said Abbie, snatching globs with her tongue the way a lizard snatches flies. The old man stared at her.

'Harold's got cholesterol,' said the lady. 'Haven't you, Harold?' The man nodded gloomily. She patted his knee. 'Time for walkies, Harold. Cheerio, dear.'

When they'd tottered off, Chester poked out of Abbie's pocket.

'Now what?' she whispered, looking round. Chester stretched towards the path on the left. Then he sank down again.

'OK,' said Abbie. She got up, slung her bag over her shoulder and headed down the path. The sun broke through, polishing the bushes either side. Abbie put her hand into her bag and fingered the tape recorder. She felt suddenly brave. She was on a story. A mission. A quest. Nothing could stop her. Nothing could scare her.

'Eek!' she squealed. Two eyes were staring over a fence. Long sad eyes in a long sad face. Abbie jumped back. The creature stumbled off, its snout wobbling.

'Very shy, tapirs.' A blonde-haired lady in green overalls was trimming the grass by the fence with long shears. 'Mind you, who wouldn't be with a hooter like that?'

Abbie laughed politely. Then she cleared her throat. 'Excuse me. Do you, um, know someone here called Coriander Platt?'

The shears went still. The lady looked up. 'No. Why do you ask?'

'I, well … nothing.'

The lady shoved the shears under her arm and hurried off.

Abbie joined a small crowd at the next fence. An elephant was curling its trunk round an iced bun. The audience clapped. It flapped its huge ears and tucked the bun into its mouth. A grey-haired keeper, whose ears were almost as impressive, held out another bun. The elephant scooped it up. Nice life, thought Abbie: eating, pooing and trumpeting all day.

A drop of rain spotted her head. The zookeeper parted with the last bun and swung his legs over the fence.

'Excuse me,' said Abbie. 'I'm looking for a lady called Cori …'

The man tugged an earlobe and rushed off.

'… ander Platt,' said Abbie to the back of his head. A shiver went through her. Did he know something? Or had he just not heard her? Unlikely, with those lugholes.

She slipped behind a tree. Unzipping her bag, she took out her tape recorder. 'MUM'S THE WORD FROM CAGEY KEEPERS,' she murmured into the microphone.

Another raindrop sank into her neck. Then another, fat and warm. Abbie hurried along the path, past giraffes who ambled round their pen like giant clockwork toys, and ostriches who sat under trees in huffy huddles. She headed for the nearest building.

It was packed inside, and very hot. Damp tourists were pushing against a low barrier that separated them from the cage. For a few minutes Abbie could see nothing but coats and hairstyles. Then she found a gap in the crowd and wormed forward to the barrier.

At the back of the cage sat an orang-utan. Its back was turned. It was making kissy faces at a tall mirror in the back wall. In its arms was a baby. The baby suddenly wriggled free and stuck out its bottom at the crowd. A golden stream arced towards them.

'Grilla dunna wee!' yelled a little girl. The mother orang turned round to the crowd. She clapped her hand over her eyes, as if to say, 'Get your species right, child.' The crowd roared. The baby orang ran along a log. Grabbing an overhead branch with its picture-hook fingers, it swung across to a pole and slid down like a fireman. It scampered to a heap of straw at the front of the cage. The straw sat up and shook itself into another orang-utan, huge and floppy. This one – Dad, no doubt – bared his teeth at the baby, as if to say, 'You ruined my nap.' Then he lay down again and covered himself with more straw. He scanned the crowd with bright, sad eyes. Abbie wasn't sure who was the audience. *He's like a kid*, she thought, *lying under a duvet and watching TV*. She suddenly felt very rude standing and staring at him. 'Sorry,' she found herself whispering. She shuffled towards the exit.

Outside the rain had stopped. Water steamed off the path. Something rustled on the left. Abbie glanced at the bushes. A pigeon fussed into the air.

She looked at her watch. Five o'clock and nothing to report but deaf zookeepers. She was getting nowhere. Might as well go home. Part of her breathed with relief: the part that liked to lie under duvets and watch TV. But another part – the part that liked to sneak into the kitchen and pinch biscuits – felt tingly and daring. And a third part – the part that felt guilty whenever she *denied* pinching biscuits – knew it would be letting Perdita down to leave now.

Something rustled again. Abbie looked down.

Not a pigeon. A hand. Attached to an arm. Beckoning.

She glanced round – there was no one about – and crouched down.

Under a pile of leaves, lying on his stomach, was a man. He lifted his head and tugged an earlobe. The elephant keeper!

'Coriander,' he mouthed.

There were footsteps behind. A family came out of the orang-utan house. Mr Big Ears shrank into the bushes. Abbie stood up.

'... picked his nose,' the little boy was saying, 'and *eated* it.'

'That's enough, Tarquin,' said his mother.

'Like this,' said the boy.

'I said that's en*ough*.'

When they'd gone Abbie crouched down again.

The grey head popped up. 'Stay,' mouthed Big Ears. 'Tonight.' He put a finger to his lips. 'Bugs.' Abbie scanned the ground for beetles.

The man shook his head and pointed up a tree. Abbie gasped. A little black box was strapped to a branch.

Two teenagers came out of the ape house. Big Ears dropped down.

'... so like, *cute*,' said the girl. She stared at Abbie, who was still crouched on the path. Abbie pretended to tie her shoelaces, remembering too late that she was wearing sandals.

The girl nudged the boy. They snickered off.

Big Ears popped out. 'Orangs,' he whispered, pointing back to the building.

A group of grown ups spilled out, chattering in a foreign language. Big Ears slid back into the undergrowth. One of the tourists smiled at Abbie.

'Looking for my, um – marbles,' she mumbled, scanning the ground. The smiling tourist nodded. Then he took out a dictionary from his rucksack.

Abbie jumped up. Where had Big Ears gone? And what had he said? 'Stay tonight,' she repeated. 'Stay. Tonight. *Stay* tonight. Stay to*night*.' No matter how she said it, the meaning didn't change.

Abbie gulped. She looked at her watch. Quarter to six. Fifteen minutes till the zoo closed. The three parts of her

– duvet-lover, biscuit-thief and valiant friend – had a little inner squabble. Duvet-lover won. Time to go home. Abbie headed for the exit. She paused to watch two seals shimmer round their pool.

A hand tapped her shoulder. And there was Big Ears again, his arm reaching out from behind a tree. 'Coriander,' he whispered. 'Prisoner … orangs. Boss –' he drew a finger across his throat. Then he snatched her wrist. He dragged her along the path to a huge wheelie bin. He lifted the lid. 'In!' he hissed, pointing behind him. Abbie heard footsteps coming down the path. So urgent was his voice and so earnest his face, she didn't think of disobeying.

Big Ears gave her a leg up. She swung one trembling leg then the other over the side of the bin. Her sandals sank into mush. Chips and cheese, sandwich and sausage: who knew what her toes were cuddling? She held her nose and tried not to think about it.

Big Ears closed the lid on her and began to pick up rubbish from the ground around the bin. He was whistling loudly. Abbie opened the lid a slit and peered through. Her throat felt dry as toast.

The blonde lady who'd been trimming the grass by the tapir pen was marching down the path. Or rather was *being* marched. By a man. Or rather a burger on legs. His white shirt and trousers met at a vast brown-belted waist, like the two halves of bun meeting the beef. But despite his width there was nothing flabby about him. Everything was neat and tight.

He stopped in front of the bin. 'Vot she look like?' His voice was high and squeaky.

'I – I can't really remember,' said the lady.

Burger Man squeezed her arm. 'But I sink you can, Dolores. Remember ve haff you on tape. Talkink.'

'Ow. Please let go Dr Klench. She – she had curly hair I think. On the plump side.'

Big-boned, thought Abbie indignantly.

Burger Man dropped Dolores' arm. He turned to Big

Ears, who'd suddenly become fascinated by the writing on a chocolate wrapper. 'Good evenink, Charlie.' Big Ears stood to attention. 'A girl iss sniffink around. You haff seen her, yess?'

'Me? Ooh no Dr Klench. I been clearing the, ah … Just a bit more, um … and I'll be heading, um … you know.'

'You are sure?' Burger Man glared at him with eyes like squashed flies.

'Me? Ooh yes Dr Klench. I haven't noticed any sniffink – I mean sniffing. And even if there um … she'll have … you know, by now.' He tapped his watch.

'Schnik!' muttered Burger Man. Abbie guessed that must be '****!!' in Burger language.

She swallowed a scream. A fat hand was coming towards the bin. It was clutching the end of an ice cream. Abbie ducked. The bin lid opened wide. There was a hard-hearted whiff of men's soap, then a soft-hearted waft of vanilla. A ball of cold hit her head.

'So Charlie,' came Burger Man's voice, 'now you come vizz me. Ve go shoppink for security cameras. Perhaps ziss girl returns tomorrow. Ve catch her on screen.'

Abbie licked the ice cream dribble from her cheek and listened to Big Ears' protests.

'Me? Ooh no, Dr Klench. Haven't quite finished, um … just wanted to, er … you know.'

'Charlie.' The voice was very calm. 'Ass Mummy used to say, I haff told you vunce. Come now.' Abbie pictured the big ears drooping. Three sets of footsteps faded down the path.

Abbie stayed there for a very long time, crouching, trembling and licking.

Her pocket wriggled. Chester crawled up her arm and onto her head. Very gently he pushed open the lid. Then he slithered out. She peered after him. There was no one about. A cloud whispered across the silver-blue sky.

Abbie hoicked herself over the side of the bin and almost fell onto the path. She brushed her sleeves and stamped the worst of the rubbish off her feet. She looked at her watch. Six twenty. The zoo must be closed. Panic bubbled in her stomach. What now? Run to the exit? What if Burger Man was waiting there? What would he do to her? Why had Charlie Big Ears helped her?

Charlie? *Ch*-arlie! Could he be the 'Ch' in Coriander's letter?

Three words danced across her brain. 'Tonight. Stay. Orangs.'

Abbie felt all wobbly. She opened her bag, took out the cell phone and dialled the Hair Museum.

'Hello?' came Perdita's breathless voice.

'I think I might be on to something,' said Abbie. 'But I've got to –' she swallowed – 'stay. Here. Tonight.'

'What?! Oh, um, hello Auntie.' Perdita's voice had gone all bright. 'It's Abbie. Yes Auntie, I'm coming. Bye then, Abbie.'

'I'll phone again,' said Abbie.

'And give my love to Ollie.' Perdita rang off.

Abbie breathed deeply … and regretted it. Salt and vinegar, meat and mould shot up her nose.

Finding a toilet block further down the path, she washed off what she could of the wheelie bin. Then she turned back towards the ape house.

***

In the kitchen on the top floor of the museum, Perdita and Matt laid the table.

'Perdie,' said Matt, 'the forks go on the left.'

'Oh, sorry Dad.' Perdita giggled and swapped them with the knives.

'They're upside down, Perdie.'

'Oops.' She giggled again.

Matt put his hand on her shoulder. 'Are you all right, darling? You seem a bit distracted this evening.'

'What? Oh, yes, just tired. I might go to bed early if that's OK.'

'Of c-course. Um, darling?'

'Yes?'

'Plates go on the table, not the floor.'

***

Coriander looked at her watch. Three and a quarter hours till her rounds. Might as well get ready. What else was there to do?

'Who wants to come with me tonight?' she asked. Vinnie, Winnie and Minnie jumped up and down. 'All right,' she laughed. 'Come and help me pack the bag.'

12

Found

The sun dropped slowly behind the high zoo wall. The air was cool and still. Darkness leaked into the sky. A star twinkled down its nose at Abbie, as if to say, 'All alone and far from home? You think *I* care?'

Abbie touched her pocket. Chester crept up her arm and snuggled against her face. But not even his talcum hug could block out the mournful smell of old dung. He settled round her neck in a comforting scarf.

There was a vending machine on the path. Abbie bought a Yorkie bar and a packet of crisps and ate them. At least you got good dinners here. She drank some more Fruits of the Forest and felt almost calm.

Something behind her squealed. She yelped.

Something ahead of her squeaked.

Something above her squawked.

And something below played the Mexican Hat Dance.

Abbie grabbed the phone. 'Hello?'

'Darling,' came Mum's faint voice. 'Everything OK? Just wanted to check.'

'Um, yes, fine,' said Abbie, remembering just in time where she was supposed to be.

'We're all missing you. Ollie doesn't know what to do with himself. I keep telling him it's only one night.' A peacock screeched. 'What on earth – ?'

'It's this crazy singer,' said Abbie, 'called, um, Peeko. Perdita loves her.'

'Oh. Right. Well, remember to clean your teeth, darling. And don't hesitate to ring if you get homesick.'

'I'll be fine, Mum,' said Abbie in a small voice. 'Bye.' She ended the call.

Homesick – as if. Homesick was for babies and woossies and … girls alone in zoos at night. Abbie suddenly longed to be at home. Sitting round the dinner table with – yes – slobbery Grandma and whiney Ollie and geeky Dad and nit-picky Mum. She gave a little sob. As if in reply, the phone blooped feebly in her hand. Oh no. Battery low. A tear ran down her cheek. Chester reached up and dabbed it off.

She sniffed. 'I'm so glad you're here, Chess.'

The phone blooped again. Putting it back in the bag, Abbie's fingers brushed the tape recorder. She brought it out and murmured into the microphone, 'HEROIC ABBIE.' That sounded good. 'HEROIC ABBIE,' she repeated, 'HEADS FOR …' For what? She bit the inside of her cheek and switched off the tape recorder.

She arrived at the Exit door of the ape house. She took

out the phone again. It had turned itself off. Panda poo. Now she was completely out of touch.

Biting her lip, she pushed the door open. Warm thick air rushed up her nose. She crept along the passage and stood in the shadows, well back from the barrier. She felt like a spy peering in at the window of a family home. The cage was dimly lit. At the back, facing the mirror with their backs turned, were the three apes.

Sorry, four.

One was wearing a light green overall and combing the hair on the baby's back. 'There,' it said. 'Last tangle gone.'

Abbie's hand flew to her mouth.

Of course Coriander didn't *really* look like an orang-utan. It was just her rust-coloured hair and her round shoulders and the shock of it all.

Something whizzed through the bars into the cage. It landed on the middle plait down Coriander's back. She whirled round. Her other two plaits whacked her in the face.

'Oh, oh, ohhhhhh!' she yelped. 'No … it can't be! *CHESTER!*'

He was all over her, jumping onto her head, cuddling her chin, tickling her cheeks. She was laughing and crying, trying to catch him. He came to rest on her shoulder.

'Chess, Chess, how did you find me?' sobbed Coriander. She buried her face in his curls. Then slowly she stood up. She took a nervous step towards the front of the cage and peered through the bars. 'Is – is anybody out there?'

From the shadows, Abbie stared at the big round face she

recognised from the photo with Abraham's beard. Coriander had oil-dark eyes like Perdita and tiny teeth like Melliflua. But there was something else about her. Something unique. A warm, exciting *orangeness*. It made Abbie think of autumn: of bonfires and pumpkin pie, choppy seas and floppy jumpers.

Abbie came forward to the barrier. 'Hello,' she said shyly. 'I'm Perdita's friend Abbie. I ... I've come to rescue you.'

Can round things get rounder? Because Coriander's eyes seemed to. She walked as if in a dream to the front of the cage. The three orangs shambled after her. They stood clasping the bars and gazing at Abbie. Who suddenly felt very silly.

A tear rolled down Coriander's cheek. Chester reached up from her shoulder to dry it.

'How – how did you find me?' Coriander's voice was low and soft. 'Where's Perdita? And Matt? Are they OK?'

Abbie assured her they were fine – or as fine as a father and daughter desperate with worry could be.

Coriander sobbed and laughed and shook her head, all at once. 'So they *do* want me back. I thought perhaps –'

'*Want* you?' Abbie burst out. 'They want nothing else! Perdita's refused to give up hope. She hasn't taken her plaits out since you left. And Mr Platt's going …' she trailed off. Perhaps 'bonkers' wasn't the most helpful word right now.

Coriander frowned. 'Then why haven't they answered my letters?'

'Because they never *got* them.' Then it all tumbled out. How Abbie had met Perdita, how they'd vowed to find Coriander, how they'd unstitched Fernando and heard his sorry tale.

Coriander listened silently, her head bowed. But when Abbie got to the part about Dirk and Melliflua hiding the letter in the Hairy Hoot she looked up sharply. Well, as sharply as someone without any sharp bits *can* look up. 'No! Why on earth would they do that?'

Abbie shrugged. She hoped that by saying nothing she'd say everything. Chester agreed by jumping through the bars onto her shoulder.

'What?' Coriander's eyebrows arched. 'You think my sister was involved with my kidnapping? That's ridiculous!' She gave a laugh – or was it a moan? 'Melliflua's devoted to us. Why else would she look after Perdita while I've been travelling? Why else would she care for her, like the mother I should have been?' She put her head in her hands. 'Ohhaaohh.' That was definitely a moan.

What is it with these Platts? thought Abbie. *No trouble believing a shrunken head can talk, but **every** trouble believing a relative's gone rotten.* 'Fernando *saw* her hide the letter,' she said gently.

Coriander shook her head. 'He must've made that up.'

'Why?'

'*I* don't know.' Coriander threw up her hands. 'Maybe he's cross with me for losing his wife's head. Maybe he wants to cause trouble.'

Maybe I'm an aardvark, thought Abbie.

'Look, dear –' Coriander had clearly finished *that* conversation – 'have you got a phone? I'm desperate to talk to them.'

Abbie winced. 'Sorry. The battery's dead. Perdita knows I'm here for the night, but that's all.'

Coriander sank against the bars. 'Oh.'

'But you'll see her soon – as soon as we've got you out of that cage.' Abbie tried to sound as if that would be the easiest thing in the world, although the thick bars and massive padlock suggested otherwise.

But ten seconds later Coriander was outside the cage, popping a big bunch of keys into her overall pocket.

'You're out!' Abbie gasped, rather unneccessarily. 'How come you've got the key?'

Coriander smiled sadly. 'I've got *all* the keys, to all the cages. Just not to the main gate. I can visit all the animals but I can't escape.'

Abbie shook her head in bewilderment.

'It's *my* turn to explain,' said Coriander. 'But first …' She leaned over the barrier and wrapped Abbie in plump arms. She smelled just like she should, of cinnamon and apples. 'You're a brave and marvellous girl, Abbie. Perdita's so lucky to have met you. Now then –' Coriander perched her not entirely small bottom on the barrier – 'let's start by introducing everyone.' She patted a spot next to her. Abbie sat down. Then Coriander beckoned to the apes.

All this time they'd been standing at the bars with their raisin eyes fixed on Abbie. Now they shambled through the open door. The two big ones crouched on the ground at Coriander's feet. The baby swung on the barrier then jumped into Coriander's lap.

'This is Minnie,' said Coriander, stroking the baby's head. Chester jumped off Abbie's shoulder and tickled Minnie's chin.

'And this is her mum Winnie.' The middle-sized orang shuffled forward and wrapped her long arms round Abbie's legs.

Coriander pointed to the biggest ape. 'And this is Vinnie, Minnie's dad.' Chester jumped onto his nose. The orang bared his teeth in a huge yawn. Chester shot off, landing in Abbie's lap.

'Don't worry, Chess,' Coriander said, laughing, 'they're the gentlest creatures. They've done nothing but kiss and cuddle me for eleven weeks.'

'You mean you've been with them all this time?' asked Abbie. 'In this cage? How come I didn't see you when I came earlier, when the zoo was open?'

Coriander pointed to the back wall of the cage. 'See that mirror? It's a door. Behind it there's a little room where I'm chained by my ankle all day. The chain lets me move round the room and use the bathroom at the back, but nothing more. So I can't get out but the orangs can come in. The zookeepers bring me food during the day. When the zoo closes at night Dr Klench comes and unchains me. Then every morning, before the zoo opens, he chains me up again.'

'Burger Man!' breathed Abbie.

Coriander chuckled: a cuddly gurgle like a kettle boiling. 'You've seen him, then.'

Abbie told her how she'd hidden in the wheelie bin. 'That man who helped me – the one with big ears – has he been smuggling out your letters?'

Coriander nodded. 'Charlie Chumb. He's posted loads of loo rolls for me. Sorry about them, by the way. They're all I had to write on. Charlie's really tried to help me. But he's terrified of Klench. They all are.'

'Who *is* Klench?' asked Abbie.

Coriander shrugged. 'Dr Hubris Klench is the zoo director. Apart from that I've no idea. Never met him before I came here.'

'So why did he kidnap you?'

'To work for him.'

'What work?'

Coriander winked at the apes. 'Shall we show her, poppets?' Vinnie whooped and clapped his hands.

'Go and get my things, would you, love?' Coriander asked Minnie. The little orang scampered to the back of the cage and pushed open the mirror door. She returned dragging a grey bag behind her.

'Thanks, Min.' Coriander slung the bag over her shoulder. Vinnie and Winnie grabbed each of her hands. Minnie climbed onto her back. 'Take the torch from the bag, dear,' she said to Abbie. 'You can light the way.'

***

Perdita opened her bedroom door. At last everyone had gone to bed. She crept across to the living-room and phoned Abbie's cell. Only to be told by a very polite lady that the number she'd dialled was unavailable, please try again later.

***

Mum sat in bed smearing moisturiser on her face. 'Abbie sounded like she was enjoying herself on the phone,' she said.

'Wonder if Matt's got any of these at the museum,' said Dad. He was thumbing through a book called *Wigs and Wildlife: Hair in the Eighteenth Century*.

'Mind you,' said Mum, blobbing white lotion on her nose, 'I don't think much of Perdita's choice in music.'

'Amazing what lived in those wigs,' said Dad.

'Peeko or something. I've never heard of her.' Mum smoothed the cream round her cheeks.

'Lice, mice …'

'Graham,' said Mum, 'are you listening?'

'… even rats.' Dad looked up. 'I know, love. It's enough to make anyone go white.'

13

~

Humming

Coriander led the way out of the ape house. Vinnie and Winnie bounced by her side, pressing their knuckles on the ground and swinging their legs through. Minnie rode on her back, clinging to her plaits.

Night had let its hair down. The darkness was broken by starlight and the beam of Abbie's torch. Chester sat on her shoulder.

After a few steps Winnie stopped. She tugged Coriander's hand and pointed at Abbie.

Coriander smiled. 'Course you can, Win.' The orang reached out her hand. Very gently Abbie took it. Winnie's fingers were cool and dry like Mum's leather gloves. Abbie felt suddenly full. As if for the first time in ages she belonged – more than that, was a vital part of things. As if she wasn't holding Winnie's hand but continuing it. As if her feet were growing from the ground and her breath was feeding the sky. As if the world was a great big dot-to-dot and she was a linking line.

Which was all very lovely. But joining dots wasn't going to free Coriander. Abbie looked up to where the charcoal smudge of wall met inky sky. It was far too high to climb over. They'd have to wait till the gates opened tomorrow. Abbie could easily hide and slip out. But Coriander? She'd be chained up in her room by then.

They stopped at the seal pool. Coriander lifted Minnie off her back and put her on the ground. The baby tumbled between her parents, who'd sat down on the path. Winnie was arranging stones in piles. Vinnie was digging in his ear and flicking its contents at the ground.

Chester jumped off Abbie's shoulder and perched on the low wall of the pool to watch.

To watch what? Abbie peered into the water, black and still.

Coriander began to hum. It was a soft sound, cool as the ocean and smooth as a squid. For a moment nothing happened. Then two sleek backs ripped the surface and two whiskery heads popped up.

'Hello, Noa,' said Coriander. 'How are you, Kaila?' She reached over and patted their heads. 'Hawaiian Monk Seals,' she said to Abbie. 'Very friendly. That's why there are only two thousand of them left. They're so easy to capture.'

The seals bobbed and coughed while Coriander reached into her bag. She brought out a pair of scissors with long blades. 'You first, Noa.'

The seal lifted his head from the water. Coriander leaned over the wall and trimmed his whiskers. 'There you go, smartiepants,' she said. Noa clapped his flippers and rolled onto his back.

'How come he lets you do that?' breathed Abbie.

'It's a trick I learned when I was diving for curly coral off Hawaii,' said Coriander. She snipped Kaila's whiskers and tickled her nose.

'So *that's* your job. Cutting the animals' hair!'

'And other things. General grooming, I suppose you'd call it. Klench must've heard about my knack of calming animals. That's why he brought me here.'

'But why kidnap you? Why not just offer you a job?'

Coriander shrugged. 'So he wouldn't have to pay me, I guess. He's the meanest man alive. The animals are half starved. And the zookeepers haven't been paid for months.'

'Why don't they leave? Or go to the police?'

Coriander shook her head. 'Search me. They seem so frightened. It's as if he's got some hold over them. Nobody talks to me except Charlie – and he only mumbles the odd word. The whole zoo's bugged, you see. Klench doesn't trust anyone.' Abbie remembered the black box in the tree. She clapped a hand to her mouth.

'Don't worry.' Coriander patted her arm. 'Charlie told me that Klench turns the microphones off at night to save money. Now,' she said, dropping the scissors into her bag, 'let's go. It's time to wake Edie up.'

Abbie would've rather let her sleep on. But Coriander insisted on tapping the glass until Edie opened a lazy eye and a very un-lazy mouth.

'Isn't she a sweetie?' Coriander undid a lock in the glass. 'Always smiling.' She slid the glass sideways. Abbie jumped back. Chester dived down her T-shirt. Minnie hopped off Coriander's back. She ran to her parents who were cowering sensibly at the door of the reptile house.

Coriander stepped into the cage. 'Want to come?'

Abbie made a sound like 'Neuthnks.'

Coriander began to hum: a rough raspy sound. Edie the crocodile wagged – or rather swiped – her tail from side to side and heaved towards Coriander. Her claws rustled over the stone floor.

Coriander tutted. 'Poor love. That must be so uncomfortable. Let's sort you out.' She crouched by the croc and patted her craggy back. Edie lifted her foot onto Coriander's lap. Abbie shrieked.

'Shh,' whispered Coriander, 'you'll scare her off.' *Good plan*, thought Abbie. But she bit her lip. Coriander was clearly in control.

She took out a pair of nail clippers from her bag and cut the croc's claws. And *then* – Abbie had to blink to make sure – Coriander brought out a little pot. The sort of little pot that perched in rows on Mum's dressing table.

'Berry blush,' said Coriander. 'Perfect for olive skin.'

'Um … why are you putting on nail varnish?' Abbie tried to sound cool.

Coriander paused mid-brush. 'Klench's orders. He wants the animals to look their best, even though he won't feed them properly.' She stroked Edie's claw and sighed. 'But how can you have good nails if you're not getting your vitamins?'

When all four feet were berry-blushed, Coriander gathered up the claw clippings and put them into her bag. 'You look like a million dollars,' she said, kissing Edie's snout. 'Probably worth it too. She's an American Crocodile,' she explained, stepping through the glass. 'Very rare. I once rode one across a swamp to get a cutting from a Frizzy Fern. Did you know that Florida's the only place in the world where you get crocs and alligators together?'

Abbie made a note to avoid Florida. Chester had clearly done the same. As soon as Coriander had shut the glass, he shot out from Abbie's T-shirt and plunged into Coriander's pocket. He brought out the bunch of keys and shoved them into her hand.

'All right, Chess, I'll lock up,' she said, laughing. 'But you can relax. Edie wouldn't hurt a fly.'

It's not flies we're worried about, thought Abbie.

Coriander fumbled with the key. Chester couldn't wait. He snatched it from her, thrust it into the keyhole and locked the cage.

Abbie stared.

Blinked.

Squeaked.

Crazy idea. Could they pull it off?

'Course we can!' cried Coriander when she'd heard the plan. 'My dear, you're a genius!'

Abbie wasn't so sure. But Coriander grabbed her hands and danced her round in a circle. 'Course we can,' she sang. 'Tremendous plan – I *know* we can!' She squeezed Abbie in her cinnamon hug. 'But first we'll need some rest. One more job then I'm done.'

It sounded simple enough. Cleaning Silvio's teeth.

Until you saw Silvio.

He was pacing about his cage. It being night, and he being nocturnal, he looked as if he could murder a good meal. Literally. The flames and coals of his baggy coat shivered as he walked. His great head was bowed. If it wasn't for all the prowling and growling, he could have been a soft toy with half its stuffing missing.

'No,' whispered Abbie. 'You can't.' But Coriander was already lifting Minnie off her back. She put her on the ground then reached for her keys. With a whimper and a wee, Minnie jumped onto her mum's back. Winnie chattered and tugged Abbie's hand, dragging her backwards down the path. Vinnie ran – or rather shuffled as fast as he could – after them. Chester covered Abbie's eyes as Coriander unlocked the cage.

The humming started. A shadowy snarl, raw as flesh and rich as blood. The orangs went quiet. Abbie lifted Chester from her eyes. She stuffed her mouth with fist. Her other hand sweated round the torch.

And there was Coriander, sitting on a rock with Silvio's head in her lap. The tiger was gazing ahead, drooling slightly, while Coriander circled a toothbrush round his teeth.

Abbie knew she'd never forget this moment. Not if all her hair and teeth *and* marbles fell out. And she knew why Perdita had never given up hope of finding her mum.

Coriander bent over the tiger. A tear fell onto his head. 'I'll miss you, Silvio,' she murmured. She stroked his ears and stood up. They walked together across the cage. Abbie could feel his purrs in her stomach. When Coriander turned the key in the lock, Silvio pressed his nose against the bars. Coriander wiped a finger across her eyes. Winnie and Vinnie took each of her hands. They returned to the ape house in silence.

Back in the cage, the orangs settled down for the night. Vinnie threw straw over himself and nestled in a corner. Winnie curled on the floor, her arms round Minnie. Coriander took Abbie's hand and led her through the mirrored door to her prison cell. It was smaller than Abbie's bedroom. A table stood against the left-hand wall. On top were arranged brushes, combs, scissors and razors. There were pots and bottles too, of shampoos and conditioners, gels and creams. Abbie guessed they were all for the animals.

In the back wall of the room was a door. 'That's the toilet,' said Coriander. 'There's a bath in there too, for the orangs and me.' Along the right-hand wall stood a bed. 'You sleep there,' Coriander insisted. 'You need to rest.' When Abbie protested she waved a hand. 'I'm too excited to sleep. I'll go and clean the orangs' cage.'

Abbie thanked her and went to sit on the bed. She nearly tripped over a little iron post on the floor. Attached to the post was a metal chain with a ring at the end like a handcuff – or rather a leg cuff.

Abbie shuddered. 'Is that what goes round your ankle?'

'What *went* round my ankle,' corrected Coriander. She kissed Abbie's cheek. 'And what'll never go round it again, thanks to you.'

Abbie sat on the bed and desperately hoped she was right.

***

Matt jumped up from his desk. He smacked his cheek. No, it wasn't a dream. That spider – right there in front of him – was carrying a box of drawing pins on its back! OK it was a small box and only five pins. But still – the spider was no bigger than his thumbnail.

'Well done, lad!' Matt didn't know if he was congratulating

the spider or himself. A few twiddles here, a few fiddles there, and the potion would be ready!

He looked at his watch. One o'clock. Better get some sleep. He'd finalise the mixture tomorrow before showing Dirk. Then he'd finish the other potions. And *then* – Matt jumped up and did a little tap dance – they'd start selling them. And the money would roll … and roll and roll! And somehow Coriander would hear, and she'd come back to help build the museum of her dreams.

Yes, yes, yes! Matt skipped across the floor, out of Hair Science and all the way upstairs to bed.

***

Mum glared into the darkness. How was she supposed to sleep with this racket going on? Dad was huffing and puffing, snorting and snuffling like a blinking rhino. She rolled over and shook his arm. 'Stop snoring, Graham,' she hissed. 'It's like a zoo in here.'

14

Schnap

*A crocodile was snapping at Abbie. A rather odd-looking crocodile, with fair hair bobbed neatly round its jaws. 'Have you cleaned your teeth?' it hissed. 'Close your mouth when you eat. You're not wearing **those** trousers.'*

*A tiny orang-utan jumped on its back, pointing at Abbie. 'It's her fault!' it shrieked, baring tiger-like fangs. '**She** took the biscuits.'*

The crocodile crawled towards her, opened its mouth and

… tickled her nose. Abbie jolted awake. One of Chester's curls was up her nostril. She removed it gently and stroked him. 'Morning Chess. You make a great pillow.'

She lay still, ticking off answers in her head. Where was she? Zoo. Why? Rescue Mission. Who? Coriander. When? Today.

Clear enough. But what about those other questions, the ones that were clouding her mind like mud in water? Had Fernando lied about Dirk and Melliflua hiding the letter?

If so, who *had* hidden it? And if Fernando *hadn't* lied, then *why* had they hidden it? Had Abbie misjudged them? Did Perdita's uncle and aunt know about Klench? Were they, like the zookeepers, terrified of him? And by saying nothing, were they just trying to protect Perdita and Matt from Klench's – well – clench? Most importantly of all, what was for breakfast?

'Nothing I'm afraid, dear,' said Coriander, when Abbie sat up in bed and asked. Coriander had taken out her plaits and was brushing her hair. It gleamed down her back like beaten copper. 'One of the zookeepers usually brings fruit at a quarter past eight, after Klench has chained me up. But not today!' She beamed. A face-filling Perdita beam, minus the piano-key teeth.

Abbie looked at her watch. Ten past seven. How was she going to survive without breakfast? As if reading her mind, Chester crawled to the foot of the bed. He rummaged in her bag and came out with the packet of Custard Creams.

'Good one,' said Abbie, grinning. She took two biscuits then offered the packet to Coriander.

'Thanks, dear.' Coriander was tying her second plait. 'I want my hair to look its best today.' When she'd finished her third plait she came over and hugged Abbie. 'I've been praying so long for this,' she said. 'I can't believe I'm actually going home.'

You're not, thought Abbie, *not yet. And the next two hours will decide if you do.* What she said, though, was, 'We'd better have a rehearsal.'

They ended up having four. The first time Winnie kept cuddling Coriander.

'You've got to give me space, poppet,' said Coriander, pushing her gently away. 'Timing is all.'

The second time Minnie peed on Chester. The weight of water slowed him down and his whizzing wasn't what it should be.

The third time Vinnie grabbed the keys from Coriander's pocket and used one to pick his nose.

The fourth time was perfect.

Abbie looked at her watch. Ten to eight. 'We'd better get into place,' she said. She kissed Coriander shyly on the cheek and Chester on the curl. 'Good luck.' Chester jumped into Coriander's pocket. Winnie and Minnie squatted in the front cage, picking out each other's fleas. Vinnie ambled into the back room and sat by the ankle chain. Coriander sat on the bed. Abbie grabbed her bag and hid behind the bathroom door. They waited in silence.

At eight o'clock oh-so-sharp came the sound of the entrance door swinging open. Then the sound of whistling. A smart, trim whistle, not a breath out of place. Then a key turning in a lock and – 'Good mornink my monkeys,' came Dr Klench's piercing voice. 'My primitif primates, my furry foolss. Do you not vish to be human like me, yess? I see you are pickink fleass, you diskustink thinks. Ass Mummy used to say, you cannot teach good breedink. But –' there was a parrot-like cackle – 'you can sell it, yess?'

Abbie peeped round the bathroom door. Dr Klench

appeared in the mirror doorway. 'Greetinks, Mrs C. And how are ve today? I see ve haff ze big buffoon in ze bedroom.' He wrinkled his nose. Abbie got the feeling that cleanliness was very dear to the heart of this white-jacketed, cream-skinned man, whose lemony hair parted in the middle and whose face was as smooth as a baby's bottom.

'A girl voss askink for you yesterday.' He smiled, or rather arranged his lips round his teeth. 'Perhaps she voss your daughter, yes? But do not fear. Today ve install cameras. Maybe soon she vill join you here in holiday home.' He cackled again.

'Dr Klench.' Abbie saw Coriander frown at him in a worried way. 'There's something wrong with Vinnie's foot. He was limping last night. I think he's got a verruca. You'll have to get some ointment.'

'Vot? I not vaste my money on silly spot creamss. Let me see.' Dr Klench tried to bend over towards Vinnie. But bending's no picnic when your waist is the size of the equator. He reached over and tried to grab Vinnie's ankle. Vinnie jerked his foot away, so that Dr Klench was pulled forward onto his knees.

Chester leapt out of Coriander's overall. Quick as a thought, he was in and out of Klench's pocket, clutching a key. Coriander grabbed the ankle ring. She clamped it round Dr Klench's surprisingly small ankle. Chester turned the key in the lock and jumped onto Abbie's shoulder.

'Vot is ziss? Get *off*!' spluttered Klench. Coriander, Vinnie and Chester jumped back to make room for his rage.

He wrenched the ankle ring, yanked the chain, went pink–red–purple in the face. 'How *dare* you? Vot iss happenink? Let me go, schnap schnap!'

Abbie dodged past the fuming football and joined the others in the doorway, beyond the reach of the ankle chain. Winnie and Minnie had come to watch. Winnie was jumping up and down and clapping. Minnie turned round,

stuck out her bottom and produced a glittering arc that landed on Klench's trousers.

'Eeuuk!' he screamed, slapping at the wee.

Vinnie dug a finger into his nose and flicked the gleaming fruit at Klench's face.

'Uueek!' he screeched, smacking at his cheek.

'Bye bye, Dr Klench,' said Coriander. She waved from the doorway. 'Thanks for having me, but I really should be getting back.'

It wasn't big and it wasn't clever. But Abbie couldn't help sticking out her tongue at the wobbling blob.

'You vill pay for ziss!' shrieked Klench. Chester was already unlocking the front of the cage with Coriander's keys.

Coriander turned to the apes. 'I'm sorry, darlings,' she said softly, 'I'll come back to help you, I promise.' There was a hairy group hug. Minnie tried to jump onto her back. Coriander passed her gently back to Winnie and locked them in the cage. They reached out their hands. She grasped them in turn. Tears glistened on her cheeks.

'It's ten past eight,' whispered Abbie. 'Five minutes till the keepers bring breakfast. We've got to go.' Chester jumped into her jacket pocket. They ran out of the ape house.

Outside, Coriander put a finger to her lips. She pointed up into a tree. Abbie nodded. Klench must have already switched on the microphones for the day.

'Stay down,' mouthed Coriander. 'Zookeepers.' Abbie crept along the path behind her, huddling close to the bushes. When they reached the seal pool they dived behind the tree where Charlie Big Ears had crouched yesterday.

'Now what?' mouthed Abbie. They could see the zoo exit gate. It was next to the entrance hut and gate only ten metres away. But it was ten metres of open ground.

Coriander squeezed Abbie's shoulder. A tall thin zookeeper was striding to the seal pool. Abbie squashed down even lower.

He put a bucket on the wall and started throwing fish into the water. 'Brekkie time, me beauties!'

Abbie heard the crash of water and saw the seals' shiny heads as they jumped for their meal. Her stomach rumbled. 'Shuddup,' she scolded it silently.

It was a big breakfast. Fish after fish gleamed out of that bucket. At last the keeper finished. He sauntered off, swinging the empty bucket. Abbie looked at her watch. Twenty past eight. Oh no. Had Klench been found?

Her question was answered by furious footsteps. Abbie looked desperately at the wheelie bin on the path, her stinky shelter of yesterday. But it would only fit one person – and anyway, it was too late. Dr Klench was by the seal pool, barking at three zookeepers. Abbie recognised Charlie and Dolores. The other one was a young man with a twitchy mouth who kept shifting from one foot to the other as if he needed the loo.

'Ze gates stay closed,' ordered Klench, 'until ve find zem. Dolores, go zat way.' He pointed left. 'Jake, over zere,' he pointed right. 'Charlie, you guard exit. I go and set up cameras schnap schnap. But first I change my vee vee trouserss. Ass Mummy vould say,' he tapped the side of his head, 'ven you stink you cannot sink.' He turned round, clicked his heels and marched back towards the ape house. The keepers peeled off to search.

Coriander stood up.

'What you doing?' mouthed Abbie, trying to pull her down.

'Charlie. He's our only hope.'

Charlie nearly tugged an ear off when he saw them. 'Can't help,' he mouthed. 'Gate locked.'

Abbie looked over at the exit gate. Tall and solid. Like the entrance gate next to it through which she'd come yesterday. How had that opened? *Think Abbie, think.*

Cigarette lady. Buzzer in the entrance hut.

They needed to get to that buzzer.

But the entrance hut was on the other side of the barred gate. The gate with gaps between the bars … *Yes!*

'Chester!' she hissed.

As if waiting for the command, he leapt out of her pocket and flew between two bars of the gate. He landed on the window of the hut. Then he wormed underneath, through the gap for pushing tickets through. Once inside he must have found the button immediately because the entrance gate began to open slowly. Chester shot out again, sailed through the gate and landed on Abbie's shoulder.

'Bye Charlie!' Coriander blew him a kiss and ran out. Abbie followed. The last thing she saw before the gate clanged shut was Charlie staring open-mouthed at her hairy shoulder and pulling on his earlobes till they reached his jaw.

***

Matt looked up from his cornflakes. 'Feeling better today, darling?

'Yes thanks, Dad.' Perdita poured milk onto the table. It dribbled over the edge.

'Rocketing rubies, watch out!' Dirk shouted, sliding his red shoes out of the way.

'Sorry Uncle.' Perdita ran for a cloth.

'Bit of a butterfingers this morning, aren't we Perdie?' Aunt Melliflua dabbed honey from her mouth with a serviette.

Matt frowned. What was up with Perdita? He caught her eye as she wiped the table. She smiled back. Maybe nothing. Maybe *he* was the distracted one. Watching that super-strong spider last night was enough to distract anyone.

'Would you like to ask Abbie round today, Perdie?' he said. That would keep her busy while he perfected the potion.

'I – I've already tried to phone her, Dad. But I can't get through.' Perdita reached for a piece of toast. A cup smashed onto the floor.

***

'I wonder what time I should go and collect Abbie,' said Mum, nibbling a Ryvita.

'Mmm?' Dad was on page seventy-eight of a book called *Noble Nicknames*. 'So that's why Ethelred was called The Unready. It's from "Unraed", which is Anglo Saxon for "can't decide".'

'I can't decide,' said Mum, licking cottage cheese off her finger, 'if it's better to go early, so she doesn't outstay her welcome. Or later, so it doesn't look as if we're dragging her away. Maybe I should give them a ring.'

'Maybe you should give them a ring,' suggested Dad. 'Mmm, I guess Alfred *must* have been Great to keep those Vikings out.'

15

Angry origami

'Two singles for Garton, please.' Abbie pushed the coins towards the bus driver.

'Hello again, love.' The driver's fringe went up – or did his face go down? 'Spent the night at the zoo, did we?' Abbie blinked. But he was grinning.

'Oh.' She grinned back. 'Yeah, sure.'

Coriander climbed onto the bus behind her. There were three other passengers sitting near the front. Abbie led the way to the back. When they'd sat down Chester crawled out of her pocket and perched on her knee.

Coriander squeezed Abbie's hand. 'I can't believe I'm going home! All thanks to you. I've never been so grateful in all my life. Not even the time a fisherman pulled me from the jaws of a shaggy-fin shark.'

Abbie blushed. 'It was nothing.'

'Nothing my follicles! Without you I'd still be in chains. My dear, with your brains and bravery, I'd take you on my travels any day.' Coriander sighed. 'Not that I'll be doing much travelling now.'

'Why not?' Abbie was horrified. Coriander without adventures would be like Superman without pants.

Coriander unbuttoned her green overall. Underneath she had on pyjamas patterned with sunflowers. *No*, thought Abbie, *has she really been wearing those ever since she was kidnapped?*

'I've been wearing these ever since I was kidnapped,' Coriander said. 'That's a long time in pyjamas. And a long time to think about what a useless mum I've been.'

'No!' Abbie bounced indignantly in her seat. Chester fell onto the floor. He wriggled back up. A piece of chewing gum was stuck to his curls.

'You're the best mum ever,' said Abbie. 'All that exploring and having adventures. I wish you were mine.'

Coriander patted her knee. 'Thank you, dear. But no you don't. Imagine a mum who's hardly ever there to brush your hair …'

Or yank your tangles, thought Abbie.

'… or buy you socks …'

Or shout at you for losing them.

'… or laugh at your jokes …'

Or never get them.

'… or wash your knickers, or empty the rubbish.'

OK. Point made.

'Imagine a mum who leaves her sister to do all those things, so she can go off gallivanting.'

*Except that **your** sister doesn't do **any** of those things*, thought Abbie. What she said, though, was, 'My mum does that stuff all the time. It's boring.'

'It doesn't have to be,' said Coriander. 'You know what? I've had so many adventures in my life. But the biggest one ever is now. Going home. Especially now I know that they want me back. And that Matt's forgiven me.'

Abbie looked at her shyly. 'I hope you don't mind me asking, but what *did* you argue about the night before you left?'

Coriander lifted Chester onto her lap. She picked off the chewing gum. He arched as a grey curl came out with it. At last she looked up. 'Well,' she said slowly, 'Matt had an idea for making money. So that we could build the museum into the most wonderful place – a world centre for all things hairy. It's always been my dream. So it was Matt's dream too. That's the sort of man he is.' Coriander's chins began to wobble. Abbie noticed what a great team they made, the second chin supporting the first like a kind cushion.

'The trouble was,' Coriander went on, 'Matt's idea wasn't a good one. In fact it was terrible – and dangerous. I couldn't agree with it. And he couldn't agree with *me*.' She sighed. 'But it's history now. Let's just forget it. Everything's going to be wonderful.'

Abbie hoped Coriander was right. That they'd go home to open arms and simple explanations. Because the alternative was doing her head in. If there *was* any funny business, how on earth would Coriander's return go down?

She sighed. There was nothing she could do about it now. Better just sit tight and think happy thoughts. And there was one sure way to do that. 'Chocky?' From her bag Abbie fished out the two King Size Mars Bars they'd bought at a corner shop before catching the bus.

Coriander gobbled hers in four bites. 'Divine. I could eat that all over again.' Chester jumped up and wiped chocolate from her mouth.

Abbie was impressed. 'My mum would freak if she knew this was my breakfast. She'd go on about spots and fillings and getting fat.'

'Well, I shall tell her how you earned your treat, freeing me from that wicked man.'

'No, you mustn't! She doesn't know anything about this trip. She thinks I've spent the night at Perdita's.'

Coriander promised to keep quiet about the rescue, even though she couldn't quite see why. 'Your mum would be so proud of you.'

Abbie snorted. 'My mum's only proud of me when I tidy my bedroom or write thank you letters. If she heard I'd spent the night in the zoo she'd kill me. Or worse,' she added darkly. 'Nope. She must never know.'

And she never would. Abbie would make sure of that. She looked at her watch. Nine fifteen. They'd be back at the museum by eleven. She'd phone home from there. Dad would come and pick her up and she'd tell the Rotten Lot all about her evening of listening to music and her morning making flapjacks with Perdita.

Coriander gazed out of the window. 'Haven't seen a lamp-post for nearly three months,' she murmured dreamily. 'Or a traffic light. And right now they're more exciting than a ride on a rhino or an ocean safari.'

For the rest of the journey Abbie listened enthralled to her travellers' tales. The rat-grey roads of England melted into orange outback as Coriander dug up the hairy tooth of the Australian Tickler, a toad that tickles flies to death in its jaws. Fields of wheat became snow as she hacked through Siberia to find the foot of a woolly mammoth. And pylons turned into pyramids as Coriander pulled three strands from the mummified armpit of the Pharaoh Cheops.

When she'd finished plaiting the fur of a platypus, Coriander got up from the seat. 'I'm going to stand by the door.'

'But we're at least three stops away,' said Abbie.

'I can't keep still.' When the bus finally drew up Abbie had to grab Coriander's arm to stop her jumping off while it was still moving.

Coriander ran down the lane that led to the Hair Museum. She waved at birds and sniffed the tiny white flowers that sprinkled the hedges. 'One thing about prison,' she called over her shoulder, 'you don't half notice things when you get out.'

Abbie followed with Chester on her shoulder. Along a bit, round the corner, over the gate and –

There were Perdita and Matt haring across the field. There were Melliflua and Dirk at the front door of the museum.

And there – *ohno* – were Mum and Dad. Standing with folded arms and folded faces like angry origami. And there too – *ohgiveusabreak* – was Ollie, jumping and waving.

The hugs, the tears, the shrieks. The laughter, the kisses, the sobs. Abbie watched as the Platts wove into each other: the big autumn lady with her wild red hair, the skinny man with the streaming face and the crazy cavorting girl.

Abbie walked slowly across the field. Chester decided to keep a low profile with Dirk and Melliflua about, and sank into her pocket. Perdita and Matt, either side of Coriander, held out their arms to Abbie.

'Our heroine!' yelled Perdita.

'Our saviour!' cried Matt.

They danced in a circle. Then Matt danced with Coriander and Perdita danced with Abbie. Then Coriander danced with Perdita and Matt danced with Abbie. Then they all danced to the museum door.

'Hello Mum,' said Abbie. Mum's face was streaked with mascara. Her left hand flew to Bob. He looked very upset, with bits of him flying in all directions.

'Hello Dad.' He looked all pink and crumpled.

'Hello Abigail,' they said together, icily.

Ollie threw himself against Abbie.

Aunt Melliflua poured into Coriander's arms. 'Corrie!' she gasped. 'I can't believe it. You're alive! We thought – we thought – didn't we, Dirkie?'

Uncle Dirk strode forward and clapped Coriander on the shoulder. 'Certainly did, old girl. Wits' end and all.' He took out a grey hanky from his grey suit pocket and blew his nose loudly.

Abbie stared at them. She'd been wrong. Fernando *had* lied. Her head swam. Why had he done it? How could Perdita forgive her for believing him? And why in the blazes were the Rotten Lot here?

'I'm sorry.' Perdita grabbed Abbie's hand. 'I had to tell

them. I was so worried about you. I couldn't get through on your mobile. Then your mum called this morning, and Auntie Mell got to the phone first.'

Melliflua let go of her sister. 'That's right, sweetie. And when I said you weren't here, your poor mother …'

'Had a fit!' said Mum. 'I didn't know what had happened to you! So we came round at once. And Perdita told us you'd –'

'Spent the night at the zoo!' cried Dad. 'Then the whole story came out, about –'

'How you'd gone missing,' said Matt, with his arms round Coriander. 'And how you hadn't contacted us. How we had no clue if you were alive or dead.' Abbie noticed that his Cs had come back with his wife.

'But my letters?' Coriander looked from Matt to Melliflua.

'Letters?' Matt frowned.

Melliflua looked bewildered. 'What letters? Look, darling, why don't you explain everything over a glass of champagne? This calls for a celebration.'

As they trooped through the front door, Mum hissed to Abbie, 'You're in big trouble, my girl. I don't care how many missing mothers you find – you lied to us!'

Ollie squeezed Abbie's hand. 'I'm glad you're back,' he said.

Melliflua led the way upstairs. 'Bit of a hike to the living area, I'm afraid. We'll pop the cork up there.'

On the first landing Abbie felt Chester slip out of her pocket. He tickled her wrist then slid down her leg and away downstairs. She couldn't help feeling relieved. Mum had enough weirdness on her plate right now without having to meet a patch of heroic chest hair.

On the second landing Matt, who hadn't let go of Coriander's hand, stopped. 'I'll be up in a minute,' he said, kissing her. 'I've got something to show you.' Smiling hugely he took a key out of his pocket and unlocked the door to Hair Science.

On the third landing Uncle Dirk took something out of *his* pocket.

Abbie's school report said she was a quick learner. But it wasn't until Dad yelled, 'What the – ?' that she realised what she was looking at.

It wasn't big. But it was very shiny. And, with a sneer that spanned his cheekbones, Dirk looked very happy to be holding it.

Melliflua opened the door to Rare Hair. 'Inside,' she hissed.

Dirk motioned everyone in with the gun. Then he took out a second one from his other pocket. 'Lock 'em in here,' he snarled, giving it to Melliflua. And with that, his pointy red shoes pattered downstairs.

* * *

Matt looked at the spider scuttling round the shoebox. One last test before he took it upstairs to show everyone. Better make sure he'd got it right. What a welcome home present for Coriander!

Matt took a glass paperweight out of his drawer. It was

twice the size of the spider. He held the creature's body gently between his finger and thumb. He lowered the paperweight onto its back. Then he let go. The paperweight scuttled round the shoebox. 'Yes!' Matt punched the air.

The door opened behind him. 'How you doing, old fruit?' came Dirk's gravelly voice.

'Fantastic!' said Matt. 'Look at this.'

Dirk gasped over his shoulder. 'Crackling crystals, it's worked! Strong as Samson!'

'Just wait till I show everyone,' giggled Matt. 'All our worries are over.'

'Oh, I wouldn't say that, old china. In fact, I'd say they were just beginning.'

Something smooth and cold tickled Matt's ear. He turned round. The end of a gun popped up his nose.

'Ullgfg,' he said.

'You finish those potions,' Dirk growled, 'and you finish 'em quick.' He reached over to the desk and snatched Matt's key to the door of Hair Science. 'Otherwise,' he snarled, backing towards the door, 'the girlies get it.' The door slammed. A key turned in the lock.

***

Back at home, Squashy Grandma's stomach growled like distant thunder. She looked at the kitchen clock. Five past twelve. Should she wait for lunch? Everyone had rushed out in such a pickle this morning. Who knew when they'd be back?

She peered into the fridge. Nice bit of chicken. Just enough for one. She took it out and popped it onto a metal tray. Bending over, she opened the oven door. 'Ooh, me lumbago.' She rubbed her back.

What was Abbie up to? Probably hiding round at Perdita's to get the wind up everyone. Grandma grinned. Just the sort of thing she'd have done at that age.

16

Bottling up

'Bags on the floor. And empty your pockets!' Melliflua waved her pistol in the dazed faces.

'Mell, what on earth – ?' began Coriander.

'I said bags down!' Melliflua pointed to a patch of floor by the door.

Abbie wished she could stop wobbling. She wobbled to the door. With wobbly hands she wobbled her overnight bag off her wobbly shoulder. Mum did the same with her handbag, adding a whimper to her wobbles.

'Pockets!' barked Melliflua. 'One at a time.'

On the floor went:

1) a big bunch of keys (Coriander)
2) three hedge trimmings (Perdita)
3) a cell phone, a pile of coins and a little book entitled *Medieval Menus* (Dad)
4) a pink comb and a tube of lipstick (Mum)

5)   a blob of plasticine and half a plastic dinosaur (Ollie, with Dad's help), and

6)   the wrapper of a King Size Mars Bar (Abbie)

'Now sit down!' The pistol trembled in Melliflua's hands.

Everyone fell on top of everyone else in their eagerness to obey. Melliflua scooped up the contents of the pockets and shoved them into Mum's handbag. Then she slung Abbie's and Mum's bags over her shoulder and stood there, pointing the pistol at the pile of prisoners. There was a long silence, broken by Mum's whimpers and Ollie's whines – or was it the other way round?

Finally Perdita said, 'W-what's going on, Auntie?'

'*I'll* tell you what!' Dirk reappeared in the doorway. He held his gun in one hand and a glass of something golden in the other. *Probably not apple juice*, thought Abbie.

'*Your* father,' he drawled at Perdita, 'is about to make *our* fortune.' He nudged Melliflua. 'He's getting somewhere with the Samson juice. I just saw a spider carry fifty times its weight!'

'Marvellous, Dirkie.' Melliflua's voice had become higher and harsher. 'And what timing! Matt has a breakthrough, Coriander walks into our arms, or rather *fire*arms –' she tittered – 'and we walk off with the potions.'

Coriander stood up. 'What potions?' she whispered.

'Down!' barked Melliflua. 'You know very well what potions.'

Coriander's hand flew to her mouth. 'You mean … ? No!

Not Matt's idea. You agreed with me it would cause nothing but trouble.'

'Trouble for you, sweetie!' Melliflua made a sound like water rushing over rocks. 'We *pretended* to agree. It was a wonderful idea! Completely wasted on you and your miserable museum. And once we'd packed you off, we got Matt working on it. He was only too glad.' She made a sound like ice being scraped off a windscreen. 'Poor Mattiepoos. He thought you'd gone off in a huffy wuffy after your argie bargie. And that he'd win you back by making money for the museum.'

Perdita stared at her aunt. 'So you *did* have Mum kidnapped,' she said softly. 'How could you Auntie?'

'Oh very easily, my sweet. Very easily indeed.' Melliflua glared at Coriander. 'I've wanted you out of my hair –' she tittered again – 'for years, you great big goodie-goodie. Perfect daughter, brilliant student, darling wife, caring friend, fearless explorer – you're enough to make a sister puke. I thought I'd seen the last of you. But thanks to Little Miss Meddler –' she scowled at Abbie then back at Coriander – 'here's your chubby mug in front of me again. But no matter.' A smile slithered across her face. 'You've made things much simpler. We can deal with you all together now, can't we, Dirkie?'

'Indeed we can,' sneered Dirk. 'And as soon as Matt's perfected a couple more potions, we'll be off down Billionaire Boulevard.' He gulped his drink and waved his gun. *Not a good combination*, thought Abbie.

162

'Potions? What potions?' cried Perdita. 'Please Mum, explain!'

'Go on, little sis,' jeered Melliflua. 'Tell her your hubbie's brainwave. Or should I say *hair*wave?'

Cut the comedy, thought Abbie, *just stick to nastiness*.

Coriander put her head in her hands. 'It's the hair,' she moaned. 'All those bits of beard and eyebrow and fringe that I've collected from famous people in history. Real hair, made of real cells. Matt figured that inside those cells must be the genes – the building blocks – of those famous people. The seeds of what made them great.'

'You mean their talents?' gasped Abbie, beginning to understand.

'You mean their abilities?' cried Dad, rethinking history lessons.

'You what?' wailed Mum.

'Their gifts, their qualities – call them what you will,' said Coriander. 'Matt thought there must be a way to extract them from the hair and –'

'Bottle them,' breathed Abbie, 'and –'

'Sell them,' said Ollie.

Everyone stared at him. It was simple. It was beautiful. A five-year-old could follow it.

'Only to help people of course,' said Coriander, her eyes brilliant with tears. 'A dose of Einstein's brains for kids at the bottom of the class. A drop of Samson's strength for those who're bullied. A dash of Helen of Troy's beauty for girls who never get dates.' She sighed. 'At least, that was Matt's plan. And all the profits would go to the museum.' She shook her head. 'But I told him he was playing with fire. That such gifts are dangerous if you don't handle them well.' Tears were tumbling down her cheeks. 'What's the good of genius if you don't use it for good? What's the sense in strength if you just beat people senseless?' She put her head in her hands. 'What if those gifts get into the wrong hands?'

'Like these, you mean?' cackled Dirk, rubbing his. 'Quivering quartz, we've got it made! Think what politicians will pay for a splash of Henry the Eighth's scheming. What crummy actresses will cough up for a bottle of Helen's beauty. What second-rate scientists will spend on a bite of Einstein's brain.' He guzzled more drink. 'We'll be dancing in dosh!' He wiggled a red shoe. 'Cavorting in cash!' He pirouetted on his points. 'Rolling in riches!' He fell forward. Melliflua grabbed his arm. Together they lurched through the doorway. There was the sound of a key in a lock followed by footsteps stumbling upstairs.

***

Down in Hair Science Matt tried to wipe his nose on the desk. But the wood was already soaked with tears. How long had he been slumped there, cursing himself? What an idiot. So blind in his eagerness to make Coriander happy – and look what he'd done!

He sat up. What *had* he done? Finished the Samson juice. But none of the others. 'And I never will,' he vowed, spreading his palms firmly on the desk. 'I'll just *pretend* to.

Because otherwise Dirk'll finish *us*.' He took a deep, brave breath. Then he burst into tears.

***

Grandma opened the oven door. What was that funny smell? She grabbed a tea towel and brought out the tray of chicken.

Oh no.

She scraped her black, singed wig off the chicken. It crumbled to ash. Must have fallen off when she put the chicken in.

Grandma sighed. Maybe she'd just have a cheese sandwich. Quarter to one. Where *were* they for Pete's sake? And why hadn't they phoned?

17

Shot!

'Oohh!' moaned Mum, leaning against the empty yeti cage. 'I'm having a nightmare. Wake me up.' When no one did, she reconsidered. 'Aahh – we're going to die!' Ollie clambered onto her lap. He buried his face in her shoulder. She clasped him close. He wiped his nose on her sleeve. 'My third best blouse!' she wailed.

Dad put his arm round her. 'Forget your blouse, Sadie. And calm down. We've got to keep our heads.'

'You right,' said a hoarse voice. 'To lose head ees no joke.'

'Fernando!' yelled Abbie. In all the excitement she'd forgotten about him. She ran over to his stand.

Perdita followed, leading Coriander by the hand. 'Fernando,' she said proudly, 'this is my mum. She rescued you from the jungle.'

He snorted. 'Rescue? She lose my ladylove!'

Coriander's smile crumpled. 'I'm so sorry,' she said softly. 'I didn't know there was a hole in my bag.'

166

There was a scream. Mum was squashed against the wall, jabbing her finger at Fernando. 'Euuchh – what is it? It's *talking*!'

Fernando wrinkled his nose at her. 'I have mouth, I have leeps – what you espect?' Mum buried her face in Dad's chest.

'Pummel the penguins,' cried Dad, 'it's a shrunken conk!'

Coriander stroked Fernando's wiry hair. 'You poor thing,' she said. 'You've been through a lot. Look at those split ends. As soon as we're out of here I'll give you a nice wash and trim.'

'Out of here? Out of here?' Mum shrieked like a parrot. 'How do we get out of here?'

Coriander went over to the snivelling heap of Mum. She knelt down and patted her arm. 'There's always a way, dear,' she said gently, fingering a plait. 'We just have to find it. Now, come and say hello.'

Coriander took Mum's hand and helped her up. She led her to the shrunken head. Dad and Ollie followed.

'Fernando,' said Coriander, 'this is Abbie's family.'

Without thinking Dad held out his hand. 'Honoured to meet you, Sir.' Fernando sniffed. Dad dropped his arm hurriedly. 'Sorry. Er, I'm Graham. This is Sadie, my wife. And my son Ollie.'

Ollie reached out and touched Fernando's nose. 'Cool,' he breathed.

Fernando's face split into a smile. 'The brother of Abbie? Then my brother too. You have fine seester. She leesten to me. She brave warrior.'

'Cool,' breathed Ollie again, fixing Abbie with wide eyes.

'Er, sorry for our rudeness,' said Dad, glancing at Mum, whose mouth was a perfect egg shape. 'Had a bit of a shock.'

'I no surprise. The Auntie-Uncle, they bad business. They … shhh!' Fernando stopped and cocked an ear. 'Here again they come. So here again I go.' His eyelids closed and his face went dead.

The barrel of a gun poked round the door. Dirk followed. He threw a bottle of water on the floor. 'That'll keep you going,' he growled. 'For now.' He turned to go. 'Oh,' he said, turning back, 'forgot to ask. Anyone hungry?'

'Me,' said Abbie automatically.

'Good!' Dirk roared with laughter and slammed the door again.

'Rats!' Abbie stamped her foot.

'Rat,' corrected Ollie. He pointed to the floor by the door.

It was more like a hairy grey footprint. Until, that is, it stood up and shook out its curls.

'Chester!' cried Abbie. Mum fainted. Dad caught her. He lowered her to the floor and sat down, cradling her head in his lap.

Chester jumped onto Abbie's shoulder. She tickled him. 'You brilliant thing,' she murmured, 'sneaking in under Dirk's shoe. Did you get flattened?' Chester stood up and puffed out his chest – if chest hair can have one. 'Now,' she continued, 'where's the door key?' Chester wriggled into a question mark.

Abbie frowned. 'What do you mean you don't know?' Chester dropped to the floor and tried to squeeze beneath her sandal.

'He means,' said Perdita, 'that it's hard to see anything when you're stuck to the bottom of a shoe.'

Abbie groaned. 'Oh great! So we'll just have to wait here for Chess to search the whole of the museum – and the whole of Dirk – till he finds the key. By which time Matt will have finished the potions and your aunt and uncle will be waltzing down Billionaire Booly-whatsit.' She plonked down onto the floor. 'And all the greedy grasping people in the world will have greedily grasped those potions. So they'll be even greedier and graspinger than before!'

'Abbie,' said Dad, 'grammar.'

'Gimme a break!' she snapped. 'Who cares about grammar when the world's about to disappear up its own … greedery? We've got to stop this. Come on everyone, think!'

Everyone did, in their own way. Coriander tugged a plait, not realising it was Perdita's. Perdita scraped her chin with her teeth. Dad stroked Mum's head and recalled great escapes in history. Fernando sang a sad serenade. Mum opened her eyes and closed them again. Ollie tickled Chester. Chester curled into a ball and bounced round Ollie's palm.

Abbie stared at him. She looked round the room, then up the wall to the high barred porthole window. 'Does that window have glass in it?' she asked, pointing.

'No,' said Perdita, 'Dad hasn't got round to it.'

'It's a long shot,' murmured Abbie. Then she explained her idea.

'Brilliant!' shouted Perdita.

'Wonderful!' cried Coriander.

'Si, si,' agreed Fernando.

'Hooray!' cheered Ollie.

'Worth a try,' said Dad.

'Mmnnff,' mumbled Mum.

Dad found a clean tissue up Mum's sleeve (Abbie was always amazed by her lack of snot). Chester found a pen by the empty yeti cage. Abbie wrote carefully on the tissue then scrunched it up. She laid it on top of Chester, who was lying flat on the floor. He curled himself round it in a ball shape.

Abbie picked him up. 'You're the coolest chest hair I've ever met,' she said.

Mum opened an eye. 'Did someone say chest hair?' She closed it, giggling hysterically.

Dad stroked Bob. 'Sssh, darling. You need to rest.' Coriander sat down next to him. He eased Mum's head gently onto her lap. Then he stood up. Chester jumped into his hand. 'Ready, old thing?' said Dad. 'Brace yourself.' He hurled the hairy ball at the window. Chester shot straight between the bars. Everyone cheered.

Coriander hugged Abbie. 'You clever thing – we're as good as free!'

Oh no we're not, thought Abbie. *You haven't met Grandma.*

***

Down in Hair Science Matt lifted the earwig out of the matchbox. 'Quick,' he whispered, putting it gently on the floor. 'Run!'

The door burst open. Dirk swaggered over, gun in hand. 'Where's my Einstein juice then?' He jabbed Matt's shoulder with the gun.

'There.' Matt pointed a trembling finger at a little brown bottle on his desk. 'I poured it on an earwig. Then I put a bit of pencil lead between its pincers. And look.'

He handed Dirk a scrap of paper. On it was written:

$$76 + \{23 + \mu\} \, \% \, \tfrac{1}{2}\Omega^3/_4{}^{\circ}{}^{\underline{a}} + 45.8/32.7 \, \S - [15*\%\,!]$$

'Sizzling sapphires!' gasped Dirk. 'You mean to say the earwig wrote this? What in the blazes does it mean?'

'It's, um, the formula for finding the circumference of an, um, elliptical, er, orbit round an, um, asteroidal, erm, electron quark. Pretty basic science.'

'I know that, you moron!' snapped Dirk, who was far

too stupid to admit he didn't understand a word. 'What I mean is what does it mean for *us*? Is the Einstein potion ready?'

'Yes,' murmured Matt.

Dirk grabbed the bottle. Then he smacked it down on the desk. 'Wait a minute! How do I know you didn't write this yourself, you pathetic pile of poop? Let me see the earwig do it.'

'Sorry.' Matt pointed to the empty matchbox. 'It worked out a formula to escape.'

***

Grandma looked up from her crossword. Ten to four and still no sign. She shook her head. Youth of today – couldn't keep time if it was nailed to their knickers.

There was a noise in the hall. At last. She shuffled out to meet the family, practising her grumpy face.

But there was no one there. Just a grey hanky with curls sticking through the letterbox. Grandma pulled it out. A crumpled tissue dropped out onto the mat. She picked it up. Neighbourhood prank. 'Very bloomin' funny,' she muttered.

Hang on a sec. Those squiggles – could they be words? Where were her glasses? Ah yes, on their chain. She hoicked them onto her nose. A sandwich crust dropped onto the floor.

Dear Grandma, she read.

We're at Perdita's museum, locked up by her aunt and uncle. They're forcing Mr Platt to make potions from famous people's hair so they can rule the world blah blah. Go to the police. Bring them here. Take Chester. But disguise him. If the police find out he's a piece of chest hair they'll freak. Quick, Grandma, our lives are in danger.

Abbie.

Grandma sighed. ''Spose the crossword can wait.' Then she looked at Chester, wriggling in her hand. 'Didn't recognise you, chuckie,' she said. 'Be a poppet and fetch me 'andbag.' Chester flew into the kitchen. He dragged her bag into the hall and slung it over her shoulder.

'Ta, love. 'Op on.' She patted her wispy head. He jumped on top. 'Snug as a bug,' she murmured, smoothing him down and shuffling out the door.

18

Waiting games

'My head,' moaned Mum. Bob rolled from side to side in Coriander's lap.

'Here, dear. Have some water.' Coriander reached for the bottle that Dirk had thrown on the floor.

'Wait,' shouted Abbie. 'It could be poison!'

Coriander nearly dropped the bottle. 'No! She wouldn't, she *couldn't*. My sister, my own flesh and blood! Who showed me how to ride a bike. Who wiped my nose. Who helped me tie my shoelaces –' Coriander paused – 'together. Who let me carry –' she frowned – '*her* bag to school.' Coriander was sounding more and more indignant. 'And clear her dishes. And tidy her room. Who taught me how to –' she jabbed the air – '*lose* at Monopoly!'

'And,' cried Abbie, relieved that Coriander might be glimpsing the truth at last, 'who kidnapped you. Who held you at gunpoint and locked you up. Oh no, she'd *never* poison your water.'

'And even if she wouldn't,' Dad continued, 'I bet her husband would.'

Fernando was nodding on his stand. 'Has husual,' he said, 'Senorita Abbie she espeak sense. Perhaps ees poison. Let me taste.'

Mum opened her eyes. 'Oh no,' she mumbled. 'Please don't risk your neck for me.' Her eyelids closed again.

Fernando snorted. 'What neck? At least I can save yours.'

Perdita crouched by the stand. 'Are you sure?' she said. The head bobbed.

'You're a hero,' said Perdita. She fetched the bottle from Coriander and held it to his puffy lips.

Abbie couldn't bear to watch. She covered her eyes with her hands.

Gulp. Glug. Gasp.

'Ees no water.'

Oh no. Abbie peeked through her fingers.

'Ees limonada.'

Everyone whooped. Perdita brought the bottle back to her mum.

'Even better,' said Coriander, holding it to Mum's lips. 'The sugar'll pep you up.'

Abbie ran over to hug Fernando – well, to grasp his ears. Ollie came and patted him. Dad tapped him on the nose with an awkward finger. 'Thanks a mil, Senor. Much obliged. And I'd love to hear about your raiding and pillaging when you have a mo.'

Mum sat up. Bob looked like an abandoned bird's nest.

'Thank you, Fernando,' she said. 'Sorry for being rude. It's just –'

'My face,' he said sadly.

'No, no,' Mum lied politely. 'It's just –' she looked round the room – 'all a bit much.' She burst into tears.

'Don't be sad, Mum,' said Ollie. He was standing by the Hairyquarium with Perdita. 'Come and see the sea horse.'

Abbie looked at him. Considering he was a prisoner in Freakville, with no food or loo, and a wet flannel for a mother, he was really doing quite well. Just for once her baby bro was acting more like a dude than doodoo.

They passed the lemonade round. 'Just a sip,' said Dad. 'Who knows when we'll get any more?' Mum sobbed even louder.

'Let's play a game,' said Coriander hurriedly.

Abbie chewed her sleeve. 'How about What's for Dinner?'

'Bacon and eggs,' said Ollie.

'Pizza and ice cream,' suggested Perdita.

'Paella e Sangria,' drooled Fernando.

'Steak and chips,' dribbled Dad.

'Sausages, mashed potato, egg, chips, chocolate mousse, cream, ice cream, Bourbons and Jammy Dodgers,' announced Abbie.

'Abigail!' Mum protested, forgetting to cry.

Coriander smiled. 'I'll have the same as Abbie. Plus a Mars Bar. And you, Sadie?'

'Tuna salad,' mumbled Mum. Everyone booed.

'Well, that was fun,' Dad sighed. 'I'm even hungrier now.'

'Hey Ollie,' said Perdita, 'want to watch a movie?'

'Ooh yes.'

Perdita ran over to the Bobus hair stand. She stood on tiptoe and switched on the video.

Mum sat up. 'Is that you?' she asked, peering at the crouching figure on the screen. Coriander nodded.

Mum's eyes widened. 'Wow. What's it like? In the jungle I mean. How do you manage?'

'Manage what?' said Coriander.

'You know. Clean underwear, make-up, that sort of thing.'

Coriander laughed. 'You rinse your knickers in jungle pools. And the rest – forget it!'

Abbie thought Mum might faint again. But to her surprise she smiled. 'How relaxing.'

'Oh it is,' said Coriander, '*that* part of it. But you miss the family so terribly. I'd rather be stuck in here with them. Oh dear,' her hand flew to her face, 'I hope Matt's all right. I wish they'd bring him up here.' She sighed. 'I s'pose they will, when they've got what they want from him.' She tugged a plait.

Mum's smile collapsed. For a moment she'd been in the jungle wringing out knickers. But the mention of Matt brought her back with a bump.

A key jiggled in the door. Melliflua glided in, gun in hand and a bucket hooked round her arm. 'Enjoying our stay, are we?' She put the bucket down. 'For your little emergencies.' She gave a little wave. 'Toodlepip, sweet peas. Oh, and sweet pees!' She tittered out of the door.

'She can't be serious!' cried Mum. 'I really need to. But I couldn't possibly. Not in that.'

'No choice,' said Dad curtly.

'Go in the corner, Mum,' said Abbie.

'Pretend you're in the jungle,' suggested Coriander, 'hiding behind a giant fern.'

'I'll look out for bottom-biting bugs,' said Perdita. She bounded round the room, peering at the ground and kicking over pretend stones.

'I'll kill the snakes!' cried Ollie. He lay on his stomach and wriggled between the stands.

'I'll beat a path,' offered Dad, hacking round the room with his imaginary machete.

Abbie snapped branches off invisible trees. 'Here's some palm leaves to wipe your –'

'All right, all right,' laughed Mum. 'But no one look.' She took the bucket. Everyone turned away. There was a teeny tinkly sound. Then she came back, smiling sheepishly.

Abbie stared. She'd never seen Mum in such a mess. Bob was clinging to one side of her head and sticking out from the other. Her face was a blotch of make-up and tears, her velvet skirt was wonky and her blouse stuck out.

'You look like a real explorer,' said Abbie.

'Me?' Mum laughed. 'I'd be eaten alive. I'm not cut out for that sort of thing.' She came over. 'Not like you, darling. You're made of sterner stuff.' She put her arm round Abbie. 'You know what? I may be in a pickle. But I'm glad I'm in a pickle with you.'

'Thanks Mum.' Abbie grinned. A day ago she couldn't have imagined anything *worse* than being locked up with the Rotten Lot. But look at them now: Mum in a mess, Dad talking raids and pillage to Fernando, and Ollie peering into the Hairy Hoot's beak. Abbie suddenly realised three things:

1)   For a Rotten Lot, they weren't really so rotten.
2)   She'd get them out of here if it was the last thing she did.
3)   If Squashy didn't come soon, it might well be.

* * *

'What are we going to do?' Matt whispered to the mouse in the shoebox. Dirk had just dumped it on the desk and insisted on seeing the effects of the Helen of Troy juice first hand.

The mouse scurried round the box. Matt's eyes scurried round his desk. A stapler, a pair of scissors, a pot of glue, some pens and an old toothbrush.

'I wonder,' he murmured. He rummaged in a drawer. Yes – a can of spray paint! He sprayed the bristles of the toothbrush

gold. Then he snipped them off. 'Keep still,' he said, grasping the mouse gently in his fist. As if understanding perfectly, the creature closed its eyes. 'That's it.' Matt squeezed a line of glue across the mouse's eyelids. Then he stuck on the golden bristles. The mouse fluttered its luscious new lashes.

'Perfect!' Matt clapped his hands. 'Now for the rest of you. I'll wash you off later, promise.'

***

At Garton police station Sergeant Bolt wiped his eyes with a hanky. 'Sorry dear, where were we?'

'Famous people's 'air,' said Grandma, glaring at him through the reception window. 'To rule the world. Look!' she pushed Abbie's tissue under the window.

The sergeant flattened it out. 'Oh yes – yes it *does* say that. I thought p'raps your specs were a bit steamed up.' He nudged the officer sitting next to him.

'It's 'er brain that's steamed up, Sarge,' whispered the young man, who had so many spots there was hardly any face.

Sergeant Bolt sucked in his cheeks. He read the rest of the letter. 'Chest hair, eh? Serious offence, you know, hairy-chested grannies. Isn't that right, Ludge?' The two officers hooted with laughter.

'I 'aven't got *chest* 'air,' snapped Grandma. 'Me friend's up 'ere, keepin' me warm. Aren't you ducks?' She patted the top of her head. Chester held his breath and tried to think like a wig.

'Her little friend up *there* needs a bit of brain surgery,' spluttered spotty Ludge.

Grandma had had enough. 'If you don't send someone out right now, I'll – I'll – write to the paper!' she shouted. 'They know me. I win all the crossword competitions. They're bound to print me.'

'OK, OK, keep your hair on. Geddit?' Sergeant Bolt whacked Ludge's arm. 'Now then –' he gulped down a giggle – 'what we'll do is we'll send someone out with you. Let me see now. How about, um …' he winked at Ludge, 'Constable Wibberly?'

'Great idea, Sarge.' Ludge bit his lip. 'She could do with some, ah … experience.'

Sergeant Bolt nodded vigorously. 'Indeed she could. Go and get her, there's a good lad. Oh, hang on a sec.' Grinning at Ludge, he brought Grandma's tissue to his nose and gave a long, loud blow.

19

Waiting pains

'… Then I put my hand into the pike's mouth,' said Coriander, 'and pulled. The hair was all tangled round its teeth.'

Mum's eyes were bigger than her face. 'Did you get bitten?'

'No. I propped the fish's mouth open with a Pikespike. That's a little stick with a fork at each end. Matt made it for me.' Coriander bit her lip. 'Oh. What are they doing to him down there?'

'How did you know the hair was from a pirate?' asked Mum. Abbie could see she was trying to distract Coriander.

'Well, I was in the Pamlico River in North Carolina. And I knew that's where Blackbeard was killed in 1718. The hair I pulled out was all black and thick, and it smelt sort of wicked. You get a feel for these things. Then when I got home we put some strands into Matt's Carbon Corkscrew to confirm the date.' Coriander put her head in her hands, 'Please just bring him here. *Please*.'

Mum squeezed her arm. 'What an exciting time you've had,' she said brightly. 'The biggest thrill *I've* had this year is stacking the dishwasher.'

'Oh but that can be fun,' said Coriander. 'So can brushing your teeth or going to the supermarket. It just depends how you do it.'

Too right, thought Abbie, picturing her treat after the weekly shop: a pot of Bio-organo-bacterio-vitaminfested yoghurt.

Mum sighed. 'S'pose so.' She looked at Dad, still chatting to Fernando – or rather nodding like a ninny at his tales of Spanish plunder. 'Do you know, I once took Graham ice skating in pyjamas?'

'What fun.' Coriander tried to sound brave. But tears had begun to trickle down her cheeks.

Perdita stopped hiding. Ollie stopped seeking. Fernando stopped talking and Dad stopped nodding. Everyone who could ran over to Coriander. Everyone who couldn't wobbled on his stand. Everyone who could sat down next to her. Everyone who couldn't sighed in Spanish sympathy. And *everyone* stared at the floor.

Where are you Chess? thought Abbie. *Where are you Squashy?*

The window filled with night. The room filled with silence. The bucket filled with wee.

***

'Where's me beauty?' barked Dirk, shoving the Hair Science door open and striding over to Matt's desk.

'Here.' Matt tilted the shoebox towards him.

'Sizzling sapphires!' Dirk jumped back from the glittering mouse. She smoothed her golden whiskers and wiggled her golden ears.

Dirk whistled. 'What a corker. Imagine *that* on two legs! Now, give me the potion.' Matt handed him a little brown pot with a white lid.

Dirk twirled round, kissing it. 'I can see those fat old frumps queuing up for their Helen juice already.'

'Just because it works on a mouse doesn't mean –' began Matt feebly.

'Oh I know old bean, I know.' Dirk nodded in mock seriousness. 'Mouse to man, that's a jolly big leap. That's why we've organised one more little test. And as soon as we know your recipes work,' he whacked Matt on the shoulder, 'I promise we'll leave you in peace.' He grinned a grim grey grin. '*Eternal* peace.' He jabbed the gun against Matt's head. 'Now get up.'

***

''Aven't a clue where we're goin',' said Grandma, shuffling along the pavement, 'but me friend knows the way.' Chester wriggled proudly on her head.

Constable Wendy Wibberly screamed. 'It's alive! What *is* it?'

'A fine 'airpiece and a trusty friend. That's all I know, and

it's all you need to. Now you just treat 'im with respect, my girl, or I'll be mentionin' a certain rude policewoman when I write to the papers.'

Wendy Wibberly bit her lip. She knew all about respect – or lack of it. Joining the police force had been the biggest mistake of her life. In her first two months she'd rescued eight cats from trees and failed three times to arrest a lad she'd caught spray painting. Not a good start. Heights made her dizzy and the boy just ran off laughing. The other policemen laughed too. At her. Her head echoed with nine weeks of snickers …

'Where's me glasses?' muttered Grandma. 'Might need 'em when we get there.'

Chester reached down and tapped a lens. 'Ooh, fancy that – I'm wearin' 'em! Glad *someone's* got eyes round 'ere.'

… Not Snickers the chocolate bar. Snickers the nasty giggles. The sort that Sergeant Bolt was probably shaking with right now, at the thought of sending her off with this barmy old bat.

'Ooh me back,' said Grandma. 'Just a little rest.' She eased herself onto a bench. ''Ow much further I wonder?'

Constable Wibberly sat down next to Grandma. She stroked a button on her jacket. Ah, the buttons. So smooth, so shiny, so calm. The whole reason she'd joined the police.

Chester jumped off Grandma's head and fussed round her lap. Then he sprang across to Constable Wibberly and tugged at her jacket. She swallowed a squeal.

'All right duckie,' said Grandma, heaving herself up. 'Keep your curls on. We're comin'.'

20

Sisters

Mum was snoring. A wire of spit gleamed down her chin. Bob was freaking out over Dad's shoulder. What a photo.

Dad was dreaming of being a conquistador. 'Take the land, spare my family,' he murmured.

Fernando was grunting gloomily.

Abbie was tickling Ollie's cheek with the Bobus hair. He'd given up laughing ages ago.

Perdita was sitting with her arms round Coriander.

Coriander was rocking back and forth, hugging her knees. 'Matt, my Matt,' she moaned. 'Matt, my Matt. Matt, my –'

The door flew open.

'MATT?!'

Matt stumbled in. Behind him came a gun. Then a sleeve. Then their hard grey owner. Behind *him* came the swish of a honey dress.

'Together at last,' snarled Dirk, punching Matt in the back. Matt toppled forward. Coriander grabbed him from the front and Perdita from the back. A Platt sandwich.

'I'm sorry,' sobbed Matt into Coriander's neck. 'I'm sorry.'

'Aaaah,' cooed Dirk, 'found your hanky at last. Now you just blow your nose on your wife and tell her how you've made our millions.'

Perdita wheeled round. 'Leave my dad alone!' She flew at Dirk. His gun went off. The bullet missed Perdita's head by a Bobus hair. It punched a hole in the Hairy Hoot's beak. Everyone screamed.

Coriander snatched Perdita to her chest. 'Darling! Are you OK?'

Melliflua shrank against the door. 'Careful, Dirkie!'

Dirk grabbed her arm. 'Shut up, woman!' He was shaking. 'Meddling mercury, that was close.' He jabbed a finger at Perdita. 'Any more nonsense, my girl, and the next one won't miss. Let's get out of here.' He clattered downstairs.

Melliflua hesitated at the door. She looked from Coriander to Perdita. Confusion glazed her amber eyes. Had the gunshot woken her up? Had it shown her that Dirk meant business? That someone in her family could actually get hurt?

Coriander stretched out her arm. 'Wait, Mell. Please.'

Melliflua snapped back into action. She whipped her gun from her pocket. 'Watch it, sis. Don't push your luck.'

Coriander sank to her knees. 'How can you do this to me?' she pleaded. 'To Perdita? After all the time you've spent looking after her?'

Not many people can snort prettily. 'Hnih!' snorted

Melliflua prettily. 'Why do you think I offered to look after her in the first place? Dirk smelt money here from the start.' Did Abbie imagine it, or was there the tiniest wobble in her voice?

Coriander must have heard it too. 'Mell,' she said, 'you've always meant so much to me. I've always looked up to you. Always admired you. Don't let it end like this!'

Melliflua's gun drooped just a little. 'Admired me? Go on.'

'Your style. Your elegance. The way you –' Coriander's hands drew circles in the air, as if trying to pluck out the right word – 'glide.'

Melliflua eyed her suspiciously.

'The way you've always, er – flossed your teeth. The way you've always, ah – plucked your eyebrows. Remember when you did mine, for my first date?'

Melliflua wrinkled her nose. 'You looked like a hedge. I couldn't let you go out like that.'

Coriander was warming up. 'The way you always, um – a'milked.'

'I what?'

'The Christmas play at school, remember? How you got to be a maid a'milking, and I was only a goose a'laying.'

Melliflua's eyes went misty. 'Such a pretty apron.'

Coriander inched closer on her knees. 'The way you've always giggled in a tinkly way.' Melliflua giggled in a tinkly way. The gun drooped a little more.

Coriander's hand reached out. 'I could never giggle like you. I could never glide or a'milk. You've always had such

189

style.' Her fingers closed round the gun. 'More than me. More than Mother.'

'Mother!' The gun jumped up. 'As if *she* cared about milk-maids or giggles! All I ever heard was, "Coriander, Coriander. *Kind* Coriander, *clever* Coriander, *cuddly* Coriander." Laying the table, fetching Father's pipe. Bounding round them like a great St Bernard. Little Goodie Two Shoes. Well now, Corrieboo, the shoes are on the other feet. It's *my* turn for glory. *You* can rot till Glory *Be!*' With a whisk of gold she was gone.

Coriander heaved herself off the floor. 'I shouldn't have mentioned Mother,' she sighed.

Fernando opened his eyes. 'A terreeble theeng, thees – how you say? – jealousy.'

'But she had nothing to be jealous of!' cried Coriander. 'She was always so glamorous. It was me who lumbered behind.'

Abbie looked at Ollie, sitting next to Mum. Could jealousy describe the urge she had to unscrew his nose whenever Mum praised him? Was jealousy what she felt every time old ladies in shops patted his head and called him an angel? Was Abbie just a mini Melliflua? Would she too grow up into a bundle of bitterness and envy? Panic shot through her. No way. Before she knew it, Abbie was crouching over her brother, hugging him from behind.

Ollie turned round. He hugged her back, smiling and surprised. 'That lady's like a creme egg,' he said, 'only backwards.'

'What do you mean?'

'She's soft on the outside, and hard on the inside.'

Even though it wasn't very funny, and even though the mention of creme eggs made her hungrier than ever, Abbie kissed his head.

***

Down in Hair Science Dirk looked at his watch. 'Tumbling topaz, where's that blasted man? I phoned him over two hours ago.'

Melliflua massaged his shoulder. 'It'll take him a while to load up. I'm sure he'll be here soon, Dirkie.'

'Don't call me that!' he snapped.

'Sorry darling.' Melliflua stuck her tongue out at the back of his head. There was no need to be so rude. She was on his side, for goodness sake. All this excitement was going to his head. And there was no need to be quite so horrid to Coriander and Perdita either. They *were* family, after all. Once Dirk had got what they wanted, he'd better leave them alone. No unnecessary violence.

A trumpet fanfare blared from Dirk's pocket. He grabbed his cell phone. 'Yes? Spot on, old fruit. I'll be right there.' He ended the call. 'He'll be at the gate in ten minutes. I'm going to wait at the door.'

***

Chester jumped onto the gate. He waited there for Grandma and Constable Wibberly, who was bringing up the rear with

191

a torch. The moon lay like a sleeping silver head between pillows of cloud.

Grandma and the constable reached the gate. There was a crackle of walkie talkie. 'Sergeant Bolt to Constable Wibberly. Do you read me?'

Wendy unclipped the machine from her belt. 'Yes Sarge,' she said in a small voice.

'All well with the female geriatric? Over.'

Why did he always speak in such a silly way over the walkie talkie? 'Yes Sarge. We're nearly at the museum. Over.'

'Good work, Wibbers,' said Bolt. Were those snorts of laughter she could hear, or just static? 'Inform us when you locate the, er, hairy miscreants,' he continued. There was a large raspberry sound. 'Over and out.'

Wendy blew a raspberry back at the machine. Then she hurled it into the darkness. She'd had enough of Bolt's cheek. As soon as she got back to the police station she was resigning.

Grandma counted the bars on the gate. 'You don't expect me to climb that, do you? I'm no streak o' bacon, you know.' Chester bounced on her head. 'Oh all right,' she sighed. 'Give us a leg up.' She waddled towards the bottom rung. Constable Wibberly bent down and cupped her hands into a step.

The sound of an engine growled up the lane. Chester whizzed off Grandma's head, grabbed her hand and pulled her behind a bush. Wendy followed. She switched off her torch as headlights ripped the darkness.

'What in 'eaven's – ?' began Grandma. Chester slammed across her mouth. They crouched behind the bush.

A van pulled up and stopped in front of the bush. The engine stuttered to silence. The beam of its headlights splashed over the gate.

A tall thin man was approaching from the other side. 'Plummeting platinum, thought you'd never get here!' he shouted to the van. He undid the padlock and opened the gate. The passenger door of the van opened. The tall thin man got in. His feet flashed red. The van bounced through the gate.

Behind the hedge Wendy Wibberly felt something brush her nose. Her buttons sagged. She knew who it was, and what he was telling her to do, even before Grandma whispered, 'After 'em.'

Wendy helped Grandma up. Without a word the old lady headed through the open gate. Wendy followed, rubbing a button with her finger. She hated the dark. But she didn't dare switch on the torch. Why oh why hadn't she taken that job polishing brassware in the church?

A cloud slid across the moon. A breeze tickled the darkness. The three pursuers trembled, shuffled and wriggled after the van, doing their best not to snivel, grunt or rustle.

The van grumbled to a stop in front of the oddest looking tower. In the frail moonlight Wendy Wibberly could almost imagine a long face with plaits either side. The van's two front doors opened. Chester dived to the left behind a bush. Wendy and Grandma lunged after him. They crouched down and peered out from a tuft that, for some strange reason, reminded Wendy of her old French teacher's hairy ears.

A short fat man got out of the driver's door. He waddled to the back of the van. The tall thin man was already there, shining a torch on the double back doors. The fat man unlocked the doors and picked up a rope from the floor inside. He pulled it. A huge white bundle fell out of the van. He yanked on the rope again. It tightened round the bundle, which squirmed and squealed on the ground.

The fat man slung the rope over his shoulder and heaved. The bundle squealed louder and wriggled in all directions. 'Help me!' he snapped. The tall man grabbed the front end of the rope. The bundle was dragged behind. The strange procession – tall man then fat man then writhing white bundle – heaved through the open door of the tower.

Wendy Wibberly stifled a scream. Poking out from beneath the bundle were at least five feet.

21

Beasts

'What's that?' Abbie put her ear to the door. Something was blundering and thundering, reeling and squealing up the stairs. It couldn't be Grandma. Not even she could manage that racket.

'Stand back!' Dad yelled just in time.

Through the door lurched Dirk. Then some rope. Then a fat man, head down and heaving. Then more rope. Then a jumble of white sheet and a stumble of brown feet. Last came Melliflua, gun in one hand, a huge padlock in the other.

'Cage!' gasped Dirk. For once he was completely out of snarl. Sweat varnished his face. Abbie was strangely comforted to note that a splinter of hair had fallen forwards, messing up his forehead.

Melliflua streamed past and opened the door of the empty yeti cage. The two men threw themselves against the gibbering white bundle, forcing it inside. Melliflua shut the door and snapped the padlock round the bars. Dirk and the fat man dropped the rope and collapsed against the bars.

Coriander shrieked. 'Klench!'

The fat man – who on closer look was extremely fat – bowed. 'I voss missink you, my dear. So ziss mornink I make small phone call to my friendss, your sister and her hussband. Zey are so glad ven I tell zem you are comink home.' He gave a fat chuckle. *The sort a doughnut would give*, thought Abbie, *if doughnuts could chuckle*.

Klench beamed. 'And now again I am free and you are captiff. Ass Mummy vould say, vot goess around comess around.'

Before Abbie could think of something witty, like 'there isn't much that goes around *you* mate', Ollie yelled, 'Rangatangs!'

He pointed at the cage. The rope had loosened and the white sheet had slipped off. And sure enough there they were, Vinnie, Winnie and Minnie, all arms and legs and gymnastic lips. When they saw Coriander their whines turned to whoops. They jabbered across the cage towards her. Winnie hugged the bars.

Coriander reached her arm through and grasped their leathery fingers. 'It's all right, my darlings. I won't let them hurt you.'

'We'll see about that.' Dirk had got his snarl back. He shoved Coriander aside and kicked the cage.

It was nerves, honest. Minnie turned round, stuck her bottom out and aimed a liquid sunbeam at Dirk's shiny red shoe.

'Beast!' roared Dirk.

'Of course she is!' cried Coriander, 'and that's how she'll stay. You start meddling with her and I'll … I'll …'

'You'll clean up this mess!' Dirk bent down and grabbed her leg. Coriander toppled over as he wiped his shoe with the hem of her pyjamas.

Matt rushed over to help her up. 'Leave her alone!' It must have been the bravest thing he'd ever whimpered.

'Oh we will, we will. It's not *her* we're interested in, you miserable mound of muck!' Dirk gave a cruel cackle. *The sort raw cabbage would give*, thought Abbie, *if raw cabbage could cackle.*

'You see,' Dirk went on, 'we met Friend Klench at a party four months ago. And when we got chatting, we discovered we had a common interest. *Money.* So when we heard Matt's

plan for the potions, we phoned Friend Klench. And we struck a little deal. Melliflua and I would – ah – *lend* your dear wife to Klench for haircutting and other duties at the zoo. And in return we'd – ah – *borrow* these hairy hobos for a few final tests. And when we've made our millions, we'll split the profits three ways. Isn't that right, woman?' Melliflua nodded so hard her gun nodded too.

A dripping black mat flew through the cage and landed on her face. 'Aarrggh!' she screamed, 'Get*off*me!'

Abbie's heart hurdled. Could it be? At last? But no. It was only yeti hair. Soaked by Minnie, thrown by Vinnie.

*Where **are** you, Chester?* Abbie wailed silently.

***

Twenty steps below, as a matter of fact. He was crawling up towards Rare Hair. Not too quickly, for two reasons:

1) Less rush more hush
2) Grandma

She was huffing and puffing as quietly as she could, which was surprisingly quietly for a world champion huffer. But there was plenty of huff inside her – the angry, indignant kind. It was brewing inside like a storm. All ready to burst on whoever it was who'd ruined her evening. Dragged away from the crossword … laughed at by those cheeky coppers … saddled with a cry-baby constable … lumbago playing up, and – what was the other thing? Oh yes – family kidnapped.

Three steps below, Constable Wibberly could almost see the old lady swelling like a balloon. Must be the bad light again.

**

Back at the police station the sergeant grabbed the walkie talkie on his desk. 'Bolt to Wibberly. Do you read me? Over.' He'd tried to contact the constable five times in the last twenty minutes. Any excuse to speak into that marvellous machine. 'Walkie talkie must be broken,' he muttered. 'Useless woman. Even technology gives up on her.'

Constable Ludge dug a finger up his left nostril. He inspected the crop and flicked it at the back of Sergeant Bolt's neck. 'Wonder what they're up to.'

A grin unfurled across the sergeant's face. 'The old bat's probably giving her a right *wigging*. Geddit?' he said, whacking Ludge's arm.

Ludge rubbed his arm and scowled. It was too late for the Sarge's painful jokes.

22

You reeker!

'Pull yourself together woman,' said Dirk, as Melliflua wiped yeti hair and orang pong off her face. 'It's only a bit of … Galloping gold! What the – ?'

'– *Blazes* d'you think you're up to?' finished a voice.

Abbie had to hand it to her. Planted in the doorway, hands on hips, she looked anything but squashy. 'Grandma!'

'Mother!' yelled Dad.

'Freeze!' roared Dirk.

Sensibly everyone froze. Everyone except Grandma, who was trembling with rage like a trifle on a tractor. 'What's all this?' she thundered. 'In all me born days … never 'eard such claptrap … potions from 'airstyles … world domination … messin' with me family … ninety-three blinkin' stairs … lumbago … no spring chicken you know … youth of today!' Or something. All in one breath.

She refuelled. ''Oo d'you think …? what's with the monkeys? … never trust a man in red shoes … game's up

maties … the Law's right be'ind me.' She swept her arm backwards in a fanfare of air. 'Law, in you come!'

The Law crept forward. It looked round, from gun to apes to people. 'Oh buttons,' it gasped, and collapsed on the floor by the door. Hartleys and Platts rushed forward to revive it.

Dr Klench was standing next to the shrunken head stand. He patted Fernando, whose face was as dead as a pan. 'Dear dear Mr Hairy Head,' he tutted. 'Ze Law iss on ze floor. I am so scared.' Then, turning to the glaring boulder in the doorway, he bowed. 'Madam.' Something like respect slid into his piggy eyes. 'You are fine voman. You remind me off my mummy. It iss sad to meet you across a gun.'

'Cut the creeping,' snapped Dirk. 'Let's get this show on the road.' He took the gun from Melliflua and led the way to the door. He jostled Grandma into the room with the gun.

'Take your 'ands off me, you brute,' she barked. 'I dunno, youth of –' she looked at his hard grey hair – 'not that *you'd* be one.'

The door slammed behind the three villains. Chester swooped down from Grandma's head and dabbed Constable Wibberly's forehead.

Mum took her hand. 'There there,' she soothed.

'It's OK,' said Dad, patting her police hat.

'No it's not,' Wendy sobbed. 'I'm useless at this stuff. I should be polishing things, not fighting crime.' Tears splashed her jacket. Chester stretched out over her buttons to keep them dry.

'Thank you,' she whispered, lying down again.

'Where's your walkie talkie?' said Abbie. 'At least we can send for help.'

'No we can't!' wailed the constable. 'I threw it away. Go on,' she urged Chester, 'rip my buttons off. It's what I deserve!'

'Rip your buttons off?' echoed Abbie. 'Now *there's* a thought.' She smiled at Wendy. 'Have you got a clean tissue?'

While Abbie organised her plan, Coriander got up and introduced the orangs to everyone. Matt held out a shy hand. Winnie seized it through the bars and drenched it in squelchy kisses. Perdita shook Vinnie's hand. Ollie came up to the cage and waved at Minnie. Minnie waved back. Ollie scratched his armpits. Minnie scratched hers. Ollie blew a raspberry. Minnie blew two.

Coriander shook the padlock. 'We've got to get them out,' she murmured to Matt in a wobbly voice, 'before the others come back and ...' she shook her head at the apes.

They seemed to understand their danger. Winnie hugged herself. Vinnie rubbed his stomach hair upwards. Minnie weed.

Matt sank against the bars. 'We'll never break that lock!' His face scrunched up. 'What have I done, Coriander? Can you ever forgive me?'

She took him in her arms. 'Of course, my darling.'

'Can you still love me?' he sniffed.

'As long as I live,' she whispered. Abbie wondered precisely how long that was going to be.

***

Down in Hair Science Dirk poured himself a third purply-red drink that probably wasn't Ribena. 'Where would 'e keep 'em,' he mumbled, 'that hopeless heap o' horse poo? Think, woman!'

'I'm looking, sweetness.' Melliflua swore at him silently and emptied another drawer.

'You reeker!' shouted Klench, from the other side of the Hair Science room.

'I wha'?' said Dirk, gulping more drink.

'I think he means Eureka,' said Melliflua.

Klench was waving a cardboard box he'd found in a cupboard. 'Yes yes, I reeka. I haff found them!' He took out three silver packets. 'Let uss go.'

***

'What on earth – ?' Sergeant Bolt stared at his desk. A hairy grey ball had just rolled under the reception window. Now it was flattening out in front of him. On top of it lay a silver button and a crumpled tissue.

'Hey Sarge,' said Ludge, peering over his shoulder, 'isn't that Wibberly's writing? What's it say?'

Bolt peered at the tissue. '*Life in danger. Send back-up to museum. W.W.*' The sergeant frowned. 'What *is* she on about? Is this some sort of joke?' He picked up the button. 'But she'd never part with this unless it was serious. How on earth did it get here?'

'The ball, Sarge?'

'You're not telling me that thing bounced all the way?' Chester jumped up and down.

'Well I'll be darned. You'd almost think it understood.'

'Sarge,' said Ludge nervously. 'I dunno how this ball thing got here. Or what it is – though come to think of it, it *does* look a bit familiar. But I reckon we've got to do something. Life in danger and all.'

Four things suddenly occurred to Sergeant Bolt:

1) Life without Dribbly Wibberly would be a lot less fun. And with no one else to tease, the other officers might turn their attention to his Santa Claus tum.

2) Wibbers was really quite a sweetie.

3) She'd had a bit of a hard time since joining up, not least from him.

4) How *could* they help her? No one knew how to find the museum.

Chester wriggled out under the window. He crawled across the floor to the door and waited.

'Get me three more officers,' commanded Sergeant Bolt. 'We're following the mop.'

23

Grabbing

Dirk stumbled through the door. His drink was in one hand, his gun in the other. He pointed the drink at the prisoners and the gun at his lips.

'Other way round, Dirkie,' hissed Melliflua behind him.

'Don' *call* me tha'!' he roared, waving the gun at her.

Klench brought up the very large rear. He waddled through the door towards the yeti cage. 'Time for treat, my darlinks,' he sang, brandishing the three silver packets at the orangs. He tore the packets and peeled them like chocolate wrappers. Except that, instead of chocolate, each packet contained something long, plastic and pointy.

'No!' screamed Coriander.

'No!' yelled Perdita.

'No!' wailed Matt.

'No!' bellowed Grandma.

'No!' shouted Abbie, Mum, Dad and Ollie. They lunged, leapt and lumbagoed at Klench.

'No,' whispered Wendy, who was still lying on the floor

near the door. She wasn't sure why the sight of a syringe had upset everyone so much. But she was keen to support her new friends.

There was a tussle and a scuffle, a whip of tough rope and a whiff of rough soap. And the next thing Abbie knew, she was part of a many-limbed monster, writhing and flailing, with a rope tightening round her middle. And Coriander's. And Perdita's. And Matt's. And Grandma's, Mum's, Dad's and Ollie's.

Quick as a ball off a bat, Klench had seized the rope that was lying on the bottom of the cage – the one that had bound the orangs – and lassoed his attackers. He would have tied up Constable Wibberly too if she'd been nearer. Now, very nimbly for a man who was taller round than up, he was circling them with the rope and pulling it tighter. Arms were pinned to sides and breaths were short. Grandma panted and ranted at Abbie's back.

'Keep still, Mother,' gasped Dad. 'The more you heave the less we breathe.'

Klench dragged the loose end of the rope to the Hairy Hoot stand. He wound it twice round the pillar then tied it in a ferocious knot. 'Ziss I should haff done before. But *your* sister,' he spat at Coriander, 'said do not bozzer.' He glared at Melliflua. 'Ass Mummy vould say, blood runss sicker zan vorter.'

'But not visky,' said Dirk, laughing so loudly you'd think it was funny. 'Well done, ol' frui.'.' He raised his glass then drained it.

'Now,' said Klench. 'Ze potions pleass.'

Dirk threw his empty glass in the air. It smashed on the floor next to Constable Wibberly, who shrieked and sat up. Dirk gave the gun to Melliflua. Then he took out three little brown bottles from his pocket. He paraded them above his head like trophies. Abbie read the labels. 'Einstein'. 'Helen'. 'Samson'. *Oh no. Oh no no no.* She tried to loosen her arms. Her hands flapped uselessly under the rope.

Dirk swayed over to Constable Wibberly and waved the bottles in her face. 'Know wha' these are, Lawlady?' She shook her head, whimpering. 'Our forshune. Our swee' smell o' success.' From the way she jerked her head back, his smell was anything but sweet.

Over by the cage Klench raised his eyebrows. Even they were overweight. 'Pleass Mr Dirk. Ve must be professional.'

Dirk swaggered towards him. 'Coming you grea' pastry.' Klench scowled and snatched the bottles from him.

The more Abbie squirmed the more the rope cut into her. She looked at the constable, still free on the floor. Their only hope. But as Wendy sat there, rubbing her buttons and sniffling, Abbie felt as much hope as a fly feels on a frog's tongue.

Klench tried to bend over to put the bottles onto the floor. But his stomach got in the way. 'You do ziss,' he snapped at Melliflua. She flowed towards him. He gave her the bottles and three syringes. She gave him the gun. Then she knelt and put the bottles and syringes onto the floor. With shaking hands she unscrewed the lid of the bottle labelled 'Einstein'.

Come on, Abbie urged herself. *Think!* She twisted her head to the right. Perdita's teeth were carving into her chin. She met Abbie's eyes and shook her head desperately.

Do something! Abbie watched Melliflua fill a syringe with the Einstein potion then lay it on the ground. Vinnie rushed to the front of the cage and stuck his arm through. But he couldn't reach the syringe. He shook the bars. Winnie waved her arms and whined. Minnie widdled in circles.

Think! Abbie twisted her head to the left. Coriander's eyes were closed. She was humming, a low sweet tune full of melon skin and bouncing branches. The apes calmed down. Vinnie sank against the bars. Minnie settled into Winnie's arms.

Use your head! Abbie looked wildly round the room. And gasped. *Or someone else's.* Someone who was winking and blinking, glaring and grimacing.

It was a chance in a million. And they'd need the police lady's help. Abbie tried to catch her eye. But it was full of buttons.

Melliflua was filling the last syringe with the Samson potion. She laid it on the ground next to the bottles of Einstein and Helen juice. Then she stood up. 'Here monkey-monkeys.' She made kissy noises. They watched her, calm and still.

'Stop humming,' hissed Abbie. 'They need to fight.' Coriander went quiet. Minnie sprang out of Winnie's arms. She began to scamper round, jabbering. Winnie chased after her while Vinnie ran round the cage in crazy loops.

Klench pointed to Dirk and Melliflua. 'Ze monkeys vill not come. You vill hold zem down.'

'You muzz be joking,' said Dirk.

'Not on your Nelly!' said Melliflua.

Klench tutted. 'Sir, I do not joke. And Madam, I haff no Nelly.' He pointed the gun at them. 'Inside!'

Melliflua fumbled in her pocket for the key. With a terrified glance at Dirk, she undid the padlock. Klench shoved them inside the cage with the gun and locked the door.

The orangs shambled over. Vinnie tried to punch Dirk. But with drunken power Dirk wrapped the gnarled fists in his own and squeezed. Gentle Vinnie, who had no idea of his own strength, yelped and collapsed on the floor.

Winnie, who knew only how to love, bless her, hugged Melliflua, who shrieked in disgust and thrust the gentle arms away. Winnie landed next to Vinnie in a heap of sweet uselessness.

Only Minnie put up a fight, gold and gushing, over grey trousers and honey dress. It wasn't much.

But it was enough.

Melliflua shrieked. Dirk roared …

… and Wendy Wibberly looked up. Her eyes met Abbie's.

'Over there,' mouthed Abbie, jerking her head towards Fernando. He winked at the constable. Wendy clapped a hand over her mouth. She stared at Abbie with eyes that were bigger than her buttons.

'Friend,' Abbie mouthed to her. 'Ball.' Understanding

crept across Wendy's face. Silently she got up and tiptoed towards the shrunken head.

Melliflua and Dirk were too busy wiping their clothes to notice. And Klench, who'd realised that little legs bend more easily than big stomachs, was approaching the floor with a straight back. He clamped the gun between his teeth, bent his knees and scooped up a syringe in each hand. Then he stood up. 'Here.' He passed a syringe through the bars to Dirk. 'You vill giff ze big monkey Einstein juice.' He gave the other syringe to Melliflua. 'You vill giff ze middle monkey Helen juice.' He took the gun from his mouth and pointed it at them.

The three apes were huddling near the back. Dirk grabbed Vinnie and pulled him forward. Melliflua grabbed Winnie. Wendy grabbed Fernando.

Dirk lifted his syringe. Melliflua lifted hers. Wendy lifted Fernando.

Dirk aimed. Melliflua aimed. Wendy aimed.

Everyone screamed.

***

Sergeant Bolt froze at the front door of the museum. He'd parked the police van by the open gate so that he and the lads could sneak after Chester across the moonlit field.

'Whassat noise?' Bolt's eyes rose up the strange tower. What on earth were those two lines, one each side of the building? They looked all sort of … twiggy. And those big things at the bottom were tied in sort of … bows. Trick of the moonlight.

Ludge banged into his back. 'It was a scream, Sarge.' He rubbed his nose – or rather the spot with nostrils in the middle of his face.

'I know that!' Sergeant Bolt shone his torch up the spiral staircase. Chester was trembling on the sixth step. Bolt pressed his walkie talkie. 'Sergeant Bolt to Constable Tring. Do you read me? Over.'

'Clear as a bell, Sarge,' came Tring's voice. 'Over.'

'Just heard piercing noise from upper regions. Ludge and I are proceeding in ascendant direction to investigate.' Bolt smiled. That sounded so much better than 'we're going upstairs'. 'What are your precise coordinates? Over.' He smiled again. Better than 'where are you?' any day.

'I'm about four steps behind you, Sarge,' said Tring. 'All due respect, but we don't really need walkie talkies. Over.'

There was a huffy pause. Then Sergeant Bolt barked into his machine, 'If I want your advice, Tring, I'll ask for it. Now get the building surrounded. Will advise you of future developments. Over and out.'

***

Constable Tring turned his walkie talkie off. 'Silly wally,' he muttered to the officer behind him. 'Why didn't he just say we'll talk later?' He gazed up at the tower and wondered what sort of hairbrush you need to plait thatch.

24

Jabbing

What had sounded to the policemen like a scream was actually seven. Rising together, in a rainbow of raucousness, were:

HORROR from Vinnie and Winnie as the syringes approached their arms,

TERROR from Wendy as she hurled Fernando towards the cage,

EXCITEMENT from Fernando as he flew there,

DELIGHT from Abbie as Fernando hit Dirk then Melliflua,

SURPRISE from Klench as the syringes whirled round in their hands,

PAIN from Dirk and Melliflua as the needles sank into *their* arms and

CONFUSION from everyone else.

'Tottering tanzanite, I've been jabbed!' bawled Dirk, lurching sideways.

'Help me!' shrieked Melliflua, clutching her arm.

'Olé!' whooped Fernando.

Dirk and Melliflua staggered round the cage. Melliflua clasped her head. Dirk grasped his throat. Melliflua moaned. Dirk groaned. It was a marvellous show. You'd think they'd been rehearsing. Then, with a last dramatic sigh they crumpled to the floor and lay still.

Klench's jaw dropped. 'Vell vell,' he gasped, scooping his voice out of his neck. 'It vould seem our guinea pigss for ze potions vill be human after all.' A smile oozed across his face. 'Most interestink.'

Something moaned at his feet. He looked down.

Fernando was rolling from side to side. 'My head. Ees pain.'

Klench's teeny eyes widened to tiny. 'Also most interestink. A talkink head.' His smile hardened. 'Ziss place iss full of vunderss. And now zey vill all be mine.'

Fernando tried to headbutt his foot. 'I espeet on your mama's castanets!' he shrieked. Klench kicked him. The head rolled towards the roped prisoners and came to rest at Abbie's feet, groaning.

Klench turned to Wendy. She was leaning against Fernando's stand, pale as a parsnip. 'Vun moof,' warned Klench, pointing the gun at her, 'and you die. Iss clear?'

'Can I nod?' she whispered.

'Yes.'

She nodded.

Vinnie, Winnie and Minnie were cowering in the corner.

They got up to investigate their new cage-mates. Dirk lay on his back. His eyes were closed and his mouth open. Melliflua curled on her side, hugging her knees. Vinnie poked her. She groaned and rolled over. Minnie scampered out of her mother's arms and onto Melliflua. She weed for joy on her new honey-coloured jungle gym.

Winnie couldn't help it. In her relief at escaping the syringe, she came towards the bars to hug Klench.

'Come darlink,' he cooed. Seizing her arm, he boinged down to the floor and up like a fat spring. And before anyone could say, 'Get-out-of-the-way-Winnie-because-that-vile-volleyball-of-a-villain-has-grabbed-the-last-syringe-and-is-about-to-inject-you-in-the-arm-with-Samson-juice' – he had.

Winnie yelped. She stumbled round the cage and sank to the floor. She lay on her back, wriggling her arms and legs like a huge hairy fly. Then she went still.

Everyone gasped. Everyone bit their lips, tongues or buttons. And everyone stared at the cage.

***

'Hang on.' Sergeant Bolt stopped on the first landing. 'What have we here?' He looked at the wonky sign over the door. 'Hairstory. What the devil's that?' Chester wriggled impatiently above him on the staircase.

'I think that mat job wants us to go upstairs Sarge,' said Ludge.

218

Sergeant Bolt tutted. 'First rule of crime-busting, Constable: check every room. Anyone could be in there, waiting to attack us from behind. Not a pleasant prospect.'

Too right, thought Ludge, eyeing his boss's behind and pitying any attacker.

Sergeant Bolt took a deep, joyful breath. Ten years of giving talks to school kids and directions to tourists – it was all worth it for this moment. He was Starsky, he was Hutch. He was The Bill. He was the whole goddamn Los Angeles Police Department. He giggled. Then turning sideways, he said, 'Brace yourself, Ludge.' He hurtled towards the door, shoulder first.

Ludge winced as the Sergeant bounced backwards, straight into his stomach.

'Don't just stand there,' barked Bolt. 'Give us a hand.'

'Sure, Sarge.' As the sergeant threw himself once more at the door, Ludge stepped forward and turned the handle. Bolt flew right through and smacked into the stomach of Henry the Eighth. The king raised his left arm above his pancake hat. 'Look out, Sarge!' Ludge yelled. The axe whirled dangerously round Bolt's head.

'Off with herrrr ...' began Henry. The axe dropped to his side.

'Outrageous!' bellowed Bolt to the king. 'You're under arrest. For assaulting a police officer and wearing a pancake in a public place.'

Ludge sighed in the doorway. 'Sarge. It's a model.'

Bolt frowned. The king frowned back. Bolt bared his

teeth. The king frowned back. Bolt blew into the royal ear. The king frowned back. 'By golly you're right,' said Bolt. 'What *is* this place?' He looked round the room. 'And who's *that*!' On the far side of the paddling pool, Helen was smiling at him. He smoothed his hair down and smiled back.

'Sarge,' sighed Ludge, 'that's a model too.'

'Supermodel, more like. Look at that hair.'

The walkie talkie burped. 'Constable Tring to Sergeant Bolt. Can you hear me Sir? Over?'

'Clear as a musical chimer, Tring, clear as a musical chimer. Over.'

'Just wondering if you've found anything, Sir. Over.'

'In a manner of speaking, Tring, in a manner. We're carrying out extensive investigations.' He winked at Helen. 'Will keep you informed of the situation, Tring. Over and out.'

Chester had run out of patience. He shot across the floor and onto Bolt's upper lip, where he twitched and tickled till the sergeant sneezed.

'All right, I'm coming,' grumbled Bolt. He came towards the door, stopping at the statue of Robin Hood. 'As soon as I've had a go with that bow and arrow.' He'd always thought of himself as a kind of Robin Hood on the beat, helping old ladies across roads and giving parking tickets to rich housewives.

***

220

Standing outside the museum Tring looked up. 'What's the old fool up to in there?' he mumbled. The lads were getting bored with playing I spy. All they could see were Bs – Bald Bushes, Bush Bunches, Bush Buns. If something didn't happen soon he'd … he'd … ooh, he'd pull the ribbons on those thatched plaits.

25

Brainy, bumpy and burly

Up in Rare Hair, something *was* happening. And something else. Two small things. An eyebrow was twitching and an eyelid was fluttering.

But what an eyebrow. And what a lid. They were changing before everyone's eyes. Dirk's brows were blossoming like brambles. Melliflua's lids were sagging like soggy teabags.

Dirk's head rolled to one side. Dandelion puff popped out of his ear. A fluffy white moustache squeezed across his upper lip. His hard grey hair was collapsing into cobwebs.

'Einstein,' breathed Matt.

You could have heard a beetle burp. Even Vinnie and Minnie, who were crouched in anguish over the sleeping Winnie, looked up.

Melliflua groaned onto her back. Her honey hair was going grey. Warts were bursting from her face. Her skin was blotching like a pavement in the rain.

'Helen?' whispered Perdita. 'But she's supposed to be –'

'Gorgeous,' sighed Dirk. He sat up and stretched his arms. 'The best sleep I've had in light years.' Then his head lolled forward. 'Aah, my brain!'

'It iss honour to meet you, Mr Albert Einstein,' said Klench, with as much awe in his voice as a foul football of a fiend can have.

Dirk looked up and frowned. The lines on his forehead wriggled like worms at a disco. 'The name's Dirkstein … I mean Eindirk.' A vagueness had crept into his gravel-grey voice. 'I mean – jiggling geometry, my head!' He clasped it in his hands.

It was Klench's turn to frown. He wheeled round to Matt. 'What haff you done? You simpleton of science! You pooper of potions!' This man is not a heap off hairy brain but a hair-brained heap off hair.'

'I – I …' said Matt unhelpfully.

'Let's try him out,' said Dad. He twisted round as far as he could inside the rope. 'What's twenty-eight times sixty-sev– ?'

'One thousand eight hundred and seventy-six,' interrupted Dirkstein, or whoever he was.

'Four hundred and fifty-nine squared?' suggested Mum.

'Two hundred and ten thousand, six hundred and eighty-one,' yawned Eindirk, or whatever.

Ollie thought of the hardest sum he could. 'Six plus six.'

Dirkstein beamed. 'Well, young man. That would be twelve the right way up, and eighteen if you turn the sixes upside down to make nines. It's all relative, you see.'

'All right Mr Smartiefart,' barked Grandma, straining

against the rope. 'What's another word for annoy? Eight letters, begins with i. That was me last crossword clue before I was so rudely dragged away.'

'Those are words, Mother, not numbers,' said Dad. 'She gets a bit mixed up,' he explained.

Dirkstein nodded in a sympathetic way. Then wished he hadn't. 'Addling algebra, my brain. It's so heavy. I can't hold it up!' He rested it against the bars of the cage and closed his eyes. 'I feel like an overripe melon.'

'Yes?' The woman lying next to him sat up. 'Did someone call me?'

'Vot – I mean *who* – are *you*?' gasped Klench, backing away from the cage.

'Mellon of Troy. I mean Helliflua. I mean – my voice – what's happened?' It had gone all squeaky.

'Forget your voice. It iss your *face* zat iss problem!' cried Klench.

'What?' Melliflua-Helen took out a powder compact from her pocket. 'Aarrghh!!' she shrieked. 'What *am* I?' For the smooth-skinned elegance of Melliflua had crumbled into a crook-nosed crone. 'But –' a memory flickered across her warts – 'I took Helen's potion. Why aren't I by*ooooo*tiful?' She put her head in her horny old hands and wailed.

'Oh Mell!' After all that had happened, Coriander couldn't help crying for her sister. 'What's happened to her, Matt?'

'I – I don't know. I must have got the potion wrong,' he said softly.

'You're telling me, you bungling birdbrain!' Mell-Hell reached her arms out to her husband. 'Oh Dirkie – how can you love me now?'

Dirkstein shrugged. That was one problem he couldn't possibly solve.

But somebody could. Lying on the floor of the cage, Winnie opened her eyes. She staggered to her feet. Hair was gushing from her body, rich and red. Nearly tripping over her tresses, she bounded over to Mell-Hell and squeezed her in loving, lumpy arms.

'Eeeuuaahh!' gasped the old prune. 'Stop … can't breathe!'

Winnie dropped her obligingly. Then she turned to hug the bars of the cage. They squashed together in her hands.

Klench pointed the gun at her. The orang reached out and curved the barrel down towards the floor. Then she took the gun from Klench and tried to peel it like a banana. When that didn't work she broke it in two.

Klench squealed. 'I vont my mummy!' Winnie picked him up in one arm and smacked a huge kiss on the duvet of his cheek. Then she dropped him. He bounced on his bottom and came to a roly-poly rest next to Mell-Hell.

Winnie ambled through the hole in the cage. Vinnie and Minnie followed, whooping and clapping.

Eindirk stayed inside, peering at the bent bars. 'Exploding exponentials,' he murmured, 'that was some force! Must be at least $(17\Pi) + (43! + 67*)$ where $*$ is strength of squeeze and … ooh, my head!' He slumped it onto a shoulder.

'Here, Winnie,' said Coriander. She began to hum: a tune of fraying ropes and freedom. Winnie ran over to the prisoners. Vinnie and Minnie followed, holding her tresses like hairy bridesmaids.

Winnie bit into the rope attached to the Hairy Hoot stand. Even her teeth were super-strong: they sliced straight through. Then, instead of lifting the rope over the prisoners, she lifted the prisoners out of the rope. They would have cheered if she wasn't squeezing them so hard. She put them down as gently as she could, which wasn't very.

Wendy ran over. Everyone slapped her on the back as if she'd just scored a goal, which in a way she had. And Fernando was kissed and held aloft like the winning ball, which in a way he was.

Coriander began to hum again: a triumphant, tie-up-the-crooks sort of tune. Winnie shambled back to the cage, her hair pouring behind like ketchup. Mell-Hell and Klench were sitting on the floor rubbing their bruises. Dirkstein was still mumbling maths inside the cage. Winnie reached inside and picked him up in one hand. She scooped up Mell-Hell in the other. With her foot she dribbled Klench like a fleshy football across the floor towards the abandoned rope. No one struggled – or if they did, no one else noticed against the Samson-like strength of Winnie. In a few seconds the orang had wound the rope round the three villains. Two of them looked very unhappy indeed.

But the third was gazing in wonder at the knot that bound him. 'Pressure must be 450 megabars, stress 133.7 … unbreakable, I'd say.'

It was the perfect moment for a policeman who'd always dreamt of arresting someone to appear in the doorway.

Sergeant Bolt appeared in the doorway.

He was wearing a green feathered cap and holding a bow and arrow.

'You're under arrest!' he shouted. He aimed the arrow at the apes, then at the people, then at the shrunken head on the floor, trying to decide who the crooks were.

Constable Ludge peered over his shoulder. He lifted the

feathered cap off Bolt's head and put it on his own. Then he doffed it at Wendy. 'Evening Wibbers.'

'Ah,' said Sergeant Bolt, spotting her, 'Constable Wibberly. I see we've arrived just in time. Don't worry, my dear, you're safe now. I've got everything under control.'

Grandma strode forward. Chester, who'd crawled into the room behind Ludge, jumped onto her head. 'Nonsense!' she bellowed. 'Poppycock and tommyrot! This young lady saved us long before *you* arrived. If it 'adn't been for 'er and that conk –' she pointed to Fernando – 'we'd be goners. I think you owe your constable an apology.'

Abbie could see the sergeant wasn't going to waste the moment on silly little sorries. He glared down at Fernando. 'You're under arrest! For ending at the neck in a public place. And *you're* under arrest,' he shouted at Mell-Hell, 'for being ugly in a public place.' She burst into tears. 'And *you're* under arrest,' he informed Klench, 'for having too much waist in a public place. And *you*,' he pointed at Winnie, 'for excess body hair in a publi–'

'Winnie!' shouted Perdita. 'What are you doing?!'

The mighty ape was pushing both hands against the circular wall of Rare Hair. The bricks were crumbling. A powdery rubble wafted to the ground.

'Oh no,' gasped Matt. 'It's the Samson juice. She's pushing the walls. Like Samson pushed the pillars in the temple of the Philistines. Sing, Coriander, sing!'

Coriander began to hum, a tune of solid walls and unbreakable bricks. But it was no good. The Samson juice was stronger than her song. Winnie couldn't stop. Another brick caved in.

Everyone who could ran towards the ape. They tugged her arms, stood on her hair, yanked and yelled. But still she pushed.

***

Which meant that no one was watching the roped prisoners. While backs were turned, Eindirk whispered something to Klench.

On a count of three, something happened. And something else. Two small things. One of them was very smelly.

A very fat man breathed in through his mouth and out through his bottom.

The rope loosened. Just a little. But enough for skinny Mell-Hell and bony Dirkstein to slip underneath it. Which left just enough slack for Klench to lift it over his head.

***

Out in the field Constable Tring jumped back. Something had landed on the grass. It was brick-shaped. Which, he realised on picking it up, was a reasonable shape to be because it was a brick. 'I spy with my little eye,' he began, 'something beginning with –' he sighed – 'B.'

'Look out!' shouted the officer next to him. Another brick thudded to the grass. Tring looked up. A third brick was hurtling from the tower. There were three brick-shaped holes in the wall.

'What the – ?' he yelled as more and more bricks popped out and plummeted. He gulped. 'I only pulled the ribbons, for Pete's sake. I had no idea this would happen.'

Three figures ran out from the bottom of the tower. (Well, two. The other one waddled quickly.) They rushed up to Tring.

'Officer!' panted the woman, whose warts were twinkling in the moonlight. 'There are three gorillas up there. They've escaped from the zoo. They're destroying the building. You've got to go up and stop them. We're going to find the zoo manager.' They dashed off.

Constable Tring gulped again. His hand moved towards his walkie talkie. Then stopped. Why hadn't Sarge contacted him? Perhaps he was lying in ape-torn shreds. Was it really wise to go up?

The walkie talkie snorted. 'Bolt to Tring. Do you read me? Over?'

'Yes Sir. You OK?' Tring's voice was wobbly.

'Well Tring. If you think that observing a hairy primate dismantle a wall while three miscreants escape behind our backs is OK – then yes, I'm one hundred per cent superdeelally. Now, I'm proceeding in a downward direction. Make sure no one leaves the building till I arrive. Over and out.'

For the third time in three minutes, Constable Tring gulped.

26

Collapse

'Everyone downstairs!' ordered Sergeant Bolt.

'But I can't leave Winnie,' wailed Coriander, clutching the ape's thick arm. Vinnie and Minnie clung on too, in a cloud of brick dust.

'Maybe she'll follow you, Mum,' shouted Perdita.

With a sob, Coriander headed to the door. Winnie looked round. Coriander reached out her hand. Her lips were moving in a last desperate hum. But it was drowned out by the rumble of crumbling tower.

Winnie stopped pushing. She looked from Coriander to the wall and back again. Another brick fell out. The floor shuddered. Coriander held out her arms. Winnie made her choice. She lumbered to the door. Vinnie and Minnie picked up her hair and followed.

Down in the field four constables staggered backwards. They fell onto the grass. They rubbed their bottoms. They shone their torches and stared at the museum door. Who could blame them? Because this is what they saw:

1) Sergeant Bolt carrying a bow and arrow,
2) Constable Ludge wearing a green feathered cap,
3) Constable Wibberly holding an oversized prune with a face,
4) an old lady wearing a wig that was jumping up and down,
5) a lady with bobbed hair that stuck out horizontally on one side,
6) a man with a beard and a bald patch carrying a bird with a tube-shaped beak,
7) a small boy holding hands with a small orang-utan,
8) a big-boned girl holding hands with a big orang-utan,
9) a lady with plaits holding hands with a very hairy orang-utan,
10) a skinny man with glasses carrying the orang-utan's hair,
11) a skinny girl with plaits carrying more of it and
12) the end of the hair, trailing along the ground.

The silent party joined the policemen. Everyone turned to watch the tower. Walls were crashing, bricks smashing. The air exploded with debris and dismay. Sofas plunged from the top floor. A paddling pool floated down. Toilet rolls and test tubes, plates and plaits, books and beards: everyday items and priceless hairy bits dived together into dust.

Coriander wailed as the Hairyquarium glittered down in a thousand raindrops. Matt moaned as the models and machines of his mind tumbled into trash. Perdita gouged her chin with her teeth and stared in wordless horror.

Was it minutes or hours they stood there? Abbie had no idea. She watched in a trance as the tower sank to its knees like a fainting giant. The roar of destruction became a grumble. Finally a pancake hat floated through the haze and settled like a lid on the mountain of rubble.

Abbie's throat clogged with sand and sobs. She reached through the soupy air and took Perdita's hand. 'At least we're all free,' she whispered. 'At least we found your mum.'

Perdita squeezed back. 'Yes,' she said. 'At least that.'

Mum put her arm round Coriander. 'Come home with us,' she said.

Dad put his arm round Matt. 'Stay as long as you like.'

Grandma put her arm round Vinnie. 'All of you.'

They followed the policemen slowly across the field. One by one they piled into the police van. Bolt radioed headquarters. 'Send two officers to Bradleigh Zoo without delay. Pursuing three suspects. 1) Unsightly female, 2) white-haired male and 3) spherical personage. Over and out.'

***

Of course none of the crooks was anywhere near the zoo. Two of them, in fact, were eight feet away from Sergeant Bolt.

'Where did Klench go?' whispered Mell-Hell as the police van roared off. She was crouching behind the bush that, a few hours ago, had been occupied by Grandma, Wendy and Chester.

'Will you shut it, woman?' muttered Eindirk. 'I'm trying to work out the diameter of the moon.'

'Well, who needs Klench? Never trusted him from the start,' murmured Mell-Hell. 'We've still got each other,' she added a little desperately. 'And a bit of money. We could go to France, Dirkie.'

'Whatever,' he mumbled.

Mell-Hell stood up. 'Come on.' She set off down the lane and forked to the right.

Three steps behind her, it suddenly occurred to Dirkstein

that the North Star was looking much prettier than his wife tonight. He forked to the left to get a better view.

***

And Klench? Well, if anyone had stopped to count, they would have noticed an extra bush in the field. A neat, tight ball, with a bun on top and two fat stems.

When the field was deserted, the bush stretched its arms. 'Schnik!' sighed Klench, gazing at the smoking remains of the museum. 'I haff lost my vunders. But at least I still haff armss and legss.' He chuckled. 'Not to mention vicked old brain. I vunder … vere iss good holiday spot for vicked old brain?' He gazed up at the moon. 'Somevere far avay. Somevere vizz much hidey holess and few personss. Persons who vill not know off my eefil doinks.' He thought for a minute. 'Off course!'

He took out the Bobus hair he'd pinched on the way out. Sell that to one of his smuggler contacts and he might have enough for the air fare.

27

Slurp

'Pass the Coco Pops,' said Grandma.

Vinnie still hadn't got the hang of it. He shoved his hand into the packet and took out five brown nuggets. He held them out in his palm to Grandma.

'Oh forget it,' she muttered and grabbed the packet from him. Vinnie liked grabbing games. He grabbed the sugar bowl and tipped it over Winnie's shaved head. Abbie giggled and helped herself to thirds.

Breakfast had been brilliant over the last three days. Because of all the visitors Mum had organised shifts:

1) Oranges
2) Children
3) Grown ups

But the children and Grandma had voted to eat with the oranges. Abbie loved watching Minnie scoop jam from the pot with her fingers. She adored the way Vinnie chomped with his mouth wide open and Winnie gobbled bananas whole. They made Abbie look like the Empress of Table Manners. How could Mum tell her off for lifting her cereal bowl to slurp the last drop of milk?

Not that Mum would, Abbie was pretty sure of that. Since they'd escaped from the museum Mum had done nothing but go on about how brave she was and who knows where they'd be without her? And that wasn't the only change. Mum had eaten a whole packet of biscuits in one go *and* worn jeans in front of the visitors.

It was like a bag had burst inside her: a bag of fun that had been tied up and shoved into a corner to make room for all the musts and shouldn'ts of motherhood – or at least, *her* kind of motherhood.

And it was another mother who'd burst it. One who used knickers (clean of course) as a shower hat to keep her plaits dry. One who was far more interested in the contents of the fridge than the colour of the kitchen. Who ate ice cream for breakfast. And who looked into Abbie's bedroom and said what a clever idea to use the floor as a wardrobe.

It was all a bit of a squeeze with the visitors. But nobody minded. Ollie was thrilled to share his room with a family of orang-utans. Vinnie and Winnie slept on a pile of cushions. A bed was made up in a pulled-out bottom drawer for Minnie. But she always ended up under the duvet with Ollie.

Perdita slept in Abbie's room. Well, not exactly slept: more like talked through the night about what had happened and what was going to.

Mum and Dad said the Platts must stay as long as they wanted. *And* that Matt and Coriander must sleep in their bedroom while they dossed down in the sitting-room. Which didn't sound like a big deal, until you realised that Mum was separated from her armoury of skin creams and perfumes. For once, though, she didn't seem bothered. She'd even started coming to breakfast without make-up on.

Chester attached himself to Grandma. Literally. He only left her head to find her things. In three days he rescued her watch from the dishwasher, her toothbrush from the garage and her slippers from the compost heap.

And Fernando? Dad asked if he'd consider dictating a book – *Heads and Tales: confessions of a conquistador.* Fernando was delighted (well, as delighted as a lovelorn head can be). He agreed to set up home in Dad's study as long as the mirror was taken out.

All in all it had been the best three days of Abbie's life. Not that she *said* that, of course, what with the Platts having lost their museum and everything. Coriander kept saying it didn't matter: all she cared about was being together again, and anyway it was only stuff.

But what stuff! All her precious hair, collected over years and continents. All Matt's inventions, created over years and workbenches. Every now and then Abbie caught Coriander gazing into space and Matt rubbing his teeth.

But neither of them complained. Matt busied himself by

quietly fixing things round the house. Abbie noticed that the sitting-room curtains were meeting for the first time in their lonely lives. And that the hall lamp was working. And that the hot tap in the kitchen no longer sounded like Grandma with the gripes.

Coriander trimmed everyone's hair. Winnie had to be shaved every morning. Thanks to the Samson juice her hair still reached her bottom by bedtime.

The orangs spent most of their time in the garden with the children. Vinnie snored in the treehouse. Winnie practised controlling her strength by hugging earthworms. At first they just squashed to goo between her finger and thumb. But by the third day she was managing to pick them up and nuzzle them against her cheek, before returning them to their relieved families. Minnie taught Ollie to dangle from the treehouse by one arm, though he never quite mastered tickling his ear with his toe.

All of which was great fun. And all of which left two questions. What had happened to the crooks, and what *would* happen to the Platts?

Part of the first answer came on the third afternoon. The phone rang. Abbie got it.

'This is Sergeant Bolt calling the Hartleys,' said the voice. 'Do you read me? Over.'

Abbie heard another voice whisper, 'It's only the phone, Sarge.'

'This is Abbie,' she said, swallowing a giggle.

'Good morning, young lady. May I speak to Mrs Platt?

Ove … I mean please.' Abbie went to call Coriander from the garden, where she was plucking Winnie's eyebrows. Matt and Perdita, who'd just rescued a hedgehog from the hedge trimmer, came inside too.

Coriander picked up the phone in the hall. 'Hello Sergeant. Any news?' she asked anxiously. After giving her statement two days ago the police had been combing the country for the crooks.

'Really?' said Coriander. 'Where? Yes, could be. I'll come as soon as I can.'

She put the phone down. 'They've arrested a man in London. He was trying to break into the Greenwich Observatory. Said he had to look through the telescope to work out the mass of Saturn's rings. Gave his name as Dirkstein or Eindirk or something but he said he couldn't be sure because he had such a headache. They're holding him at Greenwich police station. They want me to come and identify him.'

'And the other two?' asked Perdita.

Coriander sighed. 'No sign of them. I do hope Mell's all right.'

'After all she's done!' exploded Abbie. 'You're still worried about her?'

'It's just that –' Coriander shook her head – 'Melliflua's always been so proud of her looks. She'll be nothing without them. Or at least, that's what she'll think.' Coriander sat down on the bottom stair. 'I don't understand it. Winnie got Samson's strength. Dirk got Einstein's brains, even though he got a bit confused as well. But Melliflua –' she threw up her hands – 'why didn't she get Helen's beauty?'

Matt sat down next to her. 'Well. The Samson juice worked, no doubt about that. I saw the spider carry that paperweight myself. But remember I never finished the other two potions. Maybe the Einstein juice was *almost* ready but not quite. And maybe the Helen juice was miles off. Maybe I messed that one up completely.'

***

Matt was wrong about one word. 'Completely.'

The old crone bought her ferry ticket and joined the queue. A tear wove between her warts like a downhill skier. Who could blame Dirk for running away? She was a pimple on the face of the planet, a boil on the bottom of England. She, whose face was once so fine and bottom once so trim.

For the thousandth time she cursed the unfairness of it all. Dirk got brainy, the ape got strong – and she got warts. Why hadn't she inherited Helen's gift? She could never set foot in a beauty salon again. She couldn't even *talk* to anyone without them flinching. It was all her sister's fault. Why had Coriander married that idiot? He'd put the whole idea into their heads in the first place.

Mell-Hell sniffed and looked at her watch. Half an hour to boarding. To France and a new life. Where no one would know her, where she'd sneak or steal her way to a face lift.

A little boy was staring at her and whispering to his mum. Even the ferry, looming from the water, seemed to

241

be sneering down its huge rusty nose.

She gazed round the dockyard. Men in yellow jackets were driving trucks across the concrete. A crane was unloading crates from a trawler. The stink of fish, the yells of men at work – oh, it was all so dirty, so common.

Far along on the left Mell-Hell spotted a harbour where pleasure boats were moored. The yachts and speedboats glowed with wealth. That's where she should be, heading for the high life.

A horn honked. Engines juddered into life. And suddenly the ferry was heaving itself round. The water churned. Gulls shrieked in surprise. And the ferry was off, parping its oily way to France.

'Hey! I'm s'posed to be on that boat!' yelled a man with a black moustache.

'Me too!' cried a lady with a brown one. 'Here's my ticket!'

'Wait for us!' yelled a short man, brandishing a baby above his head.

'Look at the boats!' shouted his tall wife, snatching the child to safety. Every vessel in the dock, from trawlers to yachts, was heading out to sea.

***

Klench walked through the airport security arch. It beeped.

'Must be my belt buckle makink noisse,' he said to the official, whose eyebrows met in the middle.

'Step this way please, Sir.' The man ran his hands up and down – or rather round – Klench's body. 'Unbutton your shirt, please.'

'I *beck* your pardon?'

The eyebrow rose. Klench unbuttoned.

'Thank you, Sir.' The eyebrow fell. 'Just checking all that waist belongs to you. Looked as if you might be hiding something in there.'

Klench collected his shoulder bag and waddled towards the First-Class departure lounge. He took two Danish pastries from the counter and sank into an armchair. Mummy would be proud of him.

An hour later, as the plane's engines roared into life, he gave up trying to fasten his seatbelt. 'Souss America, here I come,' he giggled. 'For junkle japes and high high jinks.'

28

Deal!

It was Mum who saw it in the paper next morning. And it was Matt who put two and two together.

'Just as well I refused to go camping,' said Mum. She took a triumphant bite of Ryvita. (She'd dug her feet in a few months ago when Dad suggested a camping trip to France. He loved the idea of putting up guy ropes and groundsheets. But Mum said it would kill him and probably everyone else too, not to mention ruin her fingernails.)

Dad gulped his coffee. 'Why?'

'Look.' Mum pointed to the article.

'BOFFINS BAFFLED BY FLEEING FLEET' Dad read over her shoulder. '*Ports along the south coast of England are in turmoil after boats have been setting sail, apparently by themselves. Holidaymakers and fishermen have been stranded as hundreds of ferries, fishing trawlers and other vessels have left their harbours, some with no crew on board. Shipping experts are –*'

'Crrggh!' Matt nearly choked on his toast soldier. 'Can I see that?'

Mum gave him the paper. Matt scanned the article. Even his plaits went pale. 'I need to phone Sergeant Bolt.'

Two hours after they'd talked, the sergeant phoned back. A woman with warts had been rescued from the sea off Portsmouth. She was swimming out to a yacht. When questioned, she told the police that she was only cadging a lift because the ferry had gone without her.

'So the Helen juice *partly* worked,' said Matt, 'only *backwards*. Melliflua's face launched a thousand ships all right – but in the wrong direction. Because she went ugly instead of beautiful, they all sailed *away*!'

Abbie sucked in her cheeks. Shouldn't laugh. But after all that had happened, it did serve Melliflua a teeny bit right.

Coriander stared miserably at her boiled egg. 'So now they've got her. But how can I stand up in court and say she kidnapped me? I can't send my own sister to prison.'

'I can,' said Matt bravely.

'Me too,' said Perdita. 'She has to be locked up, Mum. So does Dirk. Otherwise we'll never be safe. Imagine how much they must hate us now. I just wish the police could find Dr Klench too.'

'Never mind 'im!' Grandma marched into the kitchen. 'Where's my Chester? I woke up this mornin' and 'e was gone.' Her hair stood up in worried wisps. ''Ow am I s'posed to find 'im, when 'e finds everything for *me*?'

'He could be out right now, finding something you've lost,' said Dad comfortingly.

Grandma gave him the look he deserved. ''Ow does that 'elp? If I've *lost* somethin', and Chester's *with* it, that just means I've lost Chester too!'

'I'll help you find him Grandma,' said Abbie, wondering if chest hair could count as a Missing Person.

An hour later the doorbell rang. And there was Chester, wiping the wellies of a man wearing a green overall and enormous ears.

'Mr Chumb!' gasped Abbie.

'Sorry to – you know.' Charlie's earlobes went red. 'This little chap … I, um, recognised him from, ah – you know. I'm, ah, looking for, um …'

Coriander was already standing in the hall with outstretched arms. 'Charlie! How wonderful. Come in.' She folded him in a huge hug. 'I was going to visit you today. How are you? And the zoo? How's everyone doing without Klench?'

His ears wiggled happily. 'Best thing that ever … sorry I didn't help you more. Owe you a – you know.'

'Nonsense! You really stuck your neck out for me. You're the only one who did. Why?'

'Ah. Long story,' said Charlie sheepishly.

Much longer than it needed to be, what with all the 'ums' and 'ahs' and 'you knows'. The potted version – the one that Abbie dictated into her tape recorder later – went like this:

MONKEY BUSINESS AT BRADLEIGH ZOO

Zookeeper Charlie Chumb has spilled the beans on crafty crook Hubris Klench. Charlie told our ace reporter Abigail Hartley how Dr Klench offered him a job six months ago. Klench promised him loadsa cash. Charlie was glad to take the job because his wife Gladys needs money for a hair transplant after a long illness. Klench also hired other keepers who needed money for sick family members. In return, Klench ordered them to keep quiet about the animal smuggling ring he was setting up. The bulging beachball of a baddie told them that he was sneaking endangered animals to the zoo from all over the world. The poor things, half starved, were to be sold on as pets. 'I knew I should tell on him,' said Charlie, adding a few 'ums' and 'ahs'. 'But I was desperate to help my Gladys.' Then Coriander Platt was kidnapped to smarten up the animals for selling on. And something snapped in Charlie Chumb. With a heart as big as his ears, he did his best to help her, behind the very wide back of cruel Klench. 'None of the keepers have been paid a penny,' said Charlie, adding a few 'you knows'. 'And Dr Klench said if we went to the police, he'd persuade them that we'd organised the smuggling ring. He's a very persuasive bloke.'

When Charlie had finished telling his tale in the sitting-room, he'd tugged his ears sadly. 'You'd better phone the – you know. Turn me in.'

Coriander jumped up and put her arm round him. 'But you saved me and all the animals!' she protested. 'If you hadn't posted my letters I'd still be in that cage. And Klench would still be up to his tricks.'

Everyone who was listening agreed that, on balance, Charlie should have told the police about Klench. (Everyone who *wasn't* listening was dozing in the treehouse, weeing on the lawn, cuddling earthworms or thinking up poems to long-lost wifeyheads.) Then everyone who was listening slapped Charlie on the back and said, never mind, he was still a hero. Then they decided that, oh dear, they might forget to tell the police about the zookeepers being in on Klench's smuggling scheme. Then Charlie burst into tears of gratitude and asked if he could have a 'quiet, um – you know' with Coriander and Matt.

While Charlie had his quiet word, Mum and Ollie prepared refreshments. It was no small task. Bourbon biscuits, chocolate muffins, bananas, melon skin, coffee, lemonade, milk and peanuts were laid out on three trays. Dad spread a cloth on the lawn. Winnie decorated the edge with earthworms.

Abbie and Perdita sat on the cloth. 'I wonder what Charlie wants to talk about with Mum and Dad,' said Perdita, plaiting three earthworms.

Abbie popped a Bourbon into her mouth and said nothing. But what she *thought* was something very exciting.

And she was right. Ten minutes later the Platt grown ups and Charlie joined them on the lawn. Coriander took one of Perdita's hands. Matt took the other. They looked at Perdita with wide, serious eyes.

'How would you feel,' said Coriander, 'about chopping raw meat?'

'And fish?' said Matt.

'About clearing panda poo?' said Coriander.

'And monkey mess?' added Matt.

'About scrubbing ellies?'

'And wearing wellies?'

'All,'

'Day,'

'Long?'

Perdita's eyebrows nearly shot off her forehead. 'The zoo?'

She whooped, she hooped, she loop-the-looped. She danced with Winnie, she pranced with Minnie. She hopped with Abbie and bopped with Ollie. Then she ran up and kissed Charlie Chumb. His ears went red and he fell over backwards, landing in a muffin.

'Your mother ...' he began, wiping chocolate off his overalls ... 'the animals, um, missed all her – you know.' He made cutting movements with his fingers.

'I bet they did,' said Perdita and kissed him again.

'And her – mmmmm,' he hummed.

'Quite,' giggled Perdita.

'And all the ...' he spread his arms in a hug.

'I understand,' said Perdita, hugging him back. His ears twitched joyfully.

Coriander beamed at them. 'So Charlie. It's a –'

'DEEEEAAAAL!!' yelled Perdita, walloping her mother in the chest.

There was loads to be done. Getting proper food for the animals for a start. The poor things had nearly starved under Klench. Meat and fruits, nuts and shoots came in by the lorry load. After that all the staff had to be paid for the six months they'd worked under Klench. And *then* there was the building of bigger and better cages, pens and pools for the animals.

Not that there was any money for all this. Klench had spent the zoo profits on tailor-made suits (OK, he didn't have much choice), barrel-loads of buns and expensive dental work (all that icing played havoc with his teeth). But when Grandma phoned the papers and the story hit the headlines, all the local businesses helped out for free.

Butchers donated meat for the big cats. Bakeries sent buns for the elephant. Fishmongers sent cod for the seals and penguins. Greengrocers supplied fruit for the monkeys and tapirs. And a local millionaire offered to fund all the building improvements.

For the rest of the summer holidays everyone was very busy.

Coriander got back to grooming the animals – sensibly this time, without nail polish for crocs or highlights for lions' manes. Charlie helped her. Mum prepared frighteningly healthy meals for all the animals.

Matt developed a mixture that made Charlie's wife's hair grow back in a week. Then he turned his skills to designing new equipment for the animals. Gina the ellie got a bun dispenser. It was like a drinks machine, with a round slot at the top. By pushing a branch into the slot with her trunk, Gina could scoop out a doughnut from a tray at the bottom. Coriander was happy for her to have box-loads of buns every day, but Mum put her foot down and said that more than four would ruin Gina's teeth. The seals got a Jacuzzi at the side of their pool. Every now and then Noa and Kaila flipped over the wall and bounced in the bubbles, clapping their flippers and giggling. And the sound of a seal giggling is enough to cheer anyone up, even a miserable shrunken head. Dad brought Fernando to watch every day after they'd worked on their book. For the tapirs Matt designed a special mirror that made their noses look shorter and boosted their confidence. Now, when anyone walked by their fence, they stuck their snouts over to be stroked. And for Silvio, Matt made a clockwork antelope that grazed round the cage and helped the tiger with pouncing practice.

Abbie and Ollie visited every day. They helped Perdita clean out the animals and play with the ones who weren't too snarly or fangy. They did such a good job that the other zoo staff decided to resign and start new careers, leaving their sad memories and shady secret behind. Abbie loved polishing the giraffes' hooves and playing hide and seek with the lemurs. And it was amazing how, with all these pets around, Ollie seemed less like one. It wasn't that she stopped arguing with him. More that they usually ended up laughing when Vinnie started copying them or Winnie hugged them or Minnie weed on their feet.

Because, of course, the orangs could no longer be caged.

Winnie would just bend the bars back and step out if she wanted a cuddle. She was actually a great help, picking Gina up when the elephant got a thorn in her foot, and lugging boulders around to make the animals' surroundings more interesting.

Although they closed the zoo for renovations, Coriander and Matt wanted to practise having visitors. So one afternoon they invited Sergeant Bolt and his constables for a guided tour. The group included Wendy Wibberly. She whispered to Abbie that she'd meant to resign, but Sarge and the lads had been so nice since that museum business she didn't have the heart to. Especially as the brass-cleaning job at the church had been taken.

The afternoon started with Grandma's Whizzy Wig Show. Chester danced on her head then disappeared down the front of her cardigan. Next thing, he was popping out of her pocket, waving Sergeant Bolt's walkie talkie.

Bolt jumped up from his seat. 'You're under arrest,' he boomed, 'for stealing police property!'

Constable Ludge turned and whacked him on the arm. It was a hard, heartfelt whack, as big as all the whacks Bolt had ever given him put together. 'Siddown, Sarge,' he ordered, with a spot-splitting grin. 'You're ruining the show.'

Chester dived into Grandma's pocket. He reappeared on her shoulder, with Ludge's spot cream held aloft. The third time he ended up on Grandma's head, brandishing a silver button from the inside of Constable Wibberly's jacket. Everyone clapped except Wendy, whose eyes filled with tears. When Chester threw the button back, however, she cheered and joined in the applause.

Grandma bowed. 'Thank you,' she tried to say. But it came out as 'Fankoo.' That was because, as she bent over, her false teeth fell out. Chester scooped them up from the ground and popped them back into place.

During the tour of the zoo Wendy Wibberly tapped Abbie on the arm. 'Is there a café here?' she murmured.

'Dr Klench ran a really grotty one,' said Abbie. 'It was more like a bus shelter. It sold stale crisps and tap water in bottles. We're going to build a proper restaurant.'

'I was wondering …' Wendy blushed. 'Do you – would you – need someone to help out? I mean polish the teapots and wipe the crockery, that sort of thing?'

So the next week Wendy handed in her (replacement) walkie talkie and said goodbye to the boys in blue. As a leaving present Bolt presented her with a framed silver button the size of a car wheel.

And so the summer passed. Mell-Hell and Dirkstein awaited trial in prison. Abbie heard from Sergeant Bolt that Mell-Hell had asked to be put in solitary confinement, and Eindirk had been allowed to paint the Milky Way on his ceiling.

But the police never found Klench. They decided he must have fled far away because wanted posters were put up all over Europe and, let's face it, he was a hard man to miss.

As August trickled into September the zoo prepared to

ASHWELL SCHOOL

open. Abbie dreaded going back to school – until Perdita announced that she'd decided to come too.

Abbie was thrilled, although she did have one slight worry. One evening, as the Hartleys and Platts were having a picnic dinner in front of Silvio's cage, Abbie asked Perdita, 'How many plaits will you wear to school?'

Perdita looked at her as if she'd just asked how many hairs a single-haired Bobus has. 'How many do you think? Three, of course.'

'Are you sure that's a good idea?' said Abbie, blushing. 'It's just that the other kids might think you're a bit – um – weird.'

'Abigail!' spluttered Mum, spitting chocolate cake over her jeans. 'Who cares? Stop worrying and have some more cake.'

MERCIER PRESS

IRISH PUBLISHER - IRISH STORY

We hope you enjoyed this book.

Since 1944, Mercier Press has published books that have been
critically important to Irish life and culture. Books that dealt with
subjects that informed readers about Irish scholars, Irish writers,
Irish history and Ireland's rich heritage.

We believe in the importance of providing accessible histories and
cultural books for all readers and all who are interested in Irish
cultural life.

Our website is the best place to find out more information about
Mercier, our books, authors, news and the best deals on a wide
variety of books. Mercier tracks the best prices for our books online
and we seek to offer the best value to our customers, offering free
delivery within Ireland.

Sign up on our website or complete and return the form below to
receive updates and special offers.

www.mercierpress.ie
www.facebook.com/mercier.press
www.twitter.com/irishpublisher

Name:

Email:

Address:

Mercier Press, Unit 3b, Oak House, Bessboro Rd, Blackrock, Cork, Ireland